What the critics have to say:

About *Moon Lust*

"Want a hot book that leaves you lusting for more? Look no further!"
- *The Best Reviews*
"An instant animal attraction"
- *Sensual Romance*
"...darkly erotic and compelling...This was my first story from Sherri L. King but it won't be my last!"
- *Sime~Gen*

About *Lune Wulf: Pack Law*

"The love scenes in this story are beyond just sizzling...they burn."
- *Mireya Orsini, Just Erotic Romance*
"Ms. O'Clare is on fire!!! Weaving together a world of werewolves that could be your neighbors, this book is well written even if it is short. It is jammed packed and very hot!"
- *Faith Jacobs, Just Erotic Romance*
"...the great beginning of new series. It's sexual and about werewolves. What more can you possible want?"
-*Patricia McGrew, Timeless Tales Romance*

About *Devlin Dynasty: Running Mate*

"...a journey of self-discovery and emotional awakenings for both the characters. It's breathtaking, energized, fast-paced and so very stimulating."
- Tracey West, Road to Romance

"...an intensely erotic story that heats the reader's blood. Despite its short length, Running Mate is a beautiful tale of love in spite of the odds."
- Meribeth McCombs, Road to Romance

About *Wolf Breeds: Wolfe's Hope*

"I cannot believe how much is packed into such a short story here. It is an intriguing and intensely erotic short story. Ms. Leigh packs a wallop in WOLFE'S HOPE."
- Robin Taylor, In The Library Reviews

"WOLFE'S HOPE is an erotic, sexually graphic read that fans of erotica and futuristic romance will enjoy."
- Janice Bennett, Sensual Romance Review

Discover for yourself why readers can't get enough of the multiple award-winning publisher Ellora's Cave. Whether you prefer e-books or paperbacks, be sure to visit EC on the web at www.ellorascave.com for an erotic reading experience that will leave you breathless.

www.ellorascave.com

PRIMAL HEAT
An Ellora's Cave Publication, May 2004

Ellora's Cave Publishing, Inc.
PO Box 787
Hudson, OH 44236-0787

ISBN #1843607409

Moon Lust © 2002 Sherri L. King
ISBN MS Reader (LIT) ISBN # 1-84360-221-0

Lunewulf: Pack Law © 2003 Lorie O'Clare
ISBN MS Reader (LIT) ISBN # 1-84360-633-X

Devlin Dynasty © 2004 Jaci Burton
ISBN MS Reader (LIT) ISBN # 1-84360-867-7

Wolf Breeds: Wolfe's Hope © 2003 Lora Leigh
ISBN MS Reader (LIT) ISBN # 1-84360-323-3

Other available formats (no ISBNs are assigned):
Adobe (PDF), Rocketbook (RB), Mobipocket (PRC) & HTML

Edited by Allie McKnight, Briana St. James, Kari Burton
Cover art by Darrell King

PRIMAL HEAT

MOON LUST
Sherri L. King

LUNEWULF: PACK LAW
Lorie O'Clare

DEVLIN DYNASTY: RUNNING MATE
Jaci Burton

WOLF BREEDS: WOLFE'S HOPE
Lora Leigh

MOON LUST

Sherri L. King

Prologue
Full Moon

Today was her birthday. As of 9:20 a.m she was no less than 32 years old. Brianna sighed, sending a puff of steam out into the frigid air. *So why am I out here, in the middle of the Ural Mountains, listening to a tour guide drone on and on about old growth forests in Russia?*

Because she'd made a promise to a dying man, that's why. Her eccentric though much beloved Uncle Alexi had always wanted to revisit the land of his birth but had never had the chance. After the death of her parents Uncle Alexi had raised her like a daughter. So for years he'd been too busy caring for her and overseeing his international forestry conservation projects to take the time for himself. As time wore on, Brianna had grown up and helped him in his conservation efforts...but he'd never found the time to get away.

He'd asked her to go in his stead.

"You must see the mountains and forests, Bri. Promise me you will go when I am gone. They are so beautiful the angels weep with envy. I want you to see them. Perhaps you will weep too, eh?" He tried to chuckle, but his body had been too weak with the cancer. He'd died that very day, but only after she'd vowed to visit his homeland.

Uncle Alexi had been right about the Middle Ural region—it was breathtaking. The air, though cold, was crisp and clean—so clear that one could see for miles in the higher regions. It was humbling to stand among the dense forest of trees as she was now, but it was also...*spooky*.

Brianna wasn't sure why the beautiful landscape should inspire such an uncomfortable fear within her — but there it was. She felt nervous, edgy. *Hunted*. As odd as it would sound to anyone else who knew her, she'd felt this way for two days now. Ever since she and the thirteen other people in her group — tourists, students, guides — had entered a particularly dense region of old growth forest.

For two days, she'd felt stalked by some unnamed fear. She could almost swear that if she turned at just the right moment she'd see a monster bearing down on her. Not even the beauty of the land and wildlife could take her mind away from that awful, hunted feeling.

It didn't help that every hour or so she caught a glimpse of something in the forest out of the corner of her eye. Like now, when something low and swift darted between the trees, obscured by the dense vegetation...

She bit her lip. Her guides had mentioned that the area was teeming with wildlife — especially foxes and wolves. Brianna found herself hoping that the shadows she so frequently saw between the trees were just the curious forest inhabitants and not the monsters of her imagination.

She blinked. "You're losing it," she murmured to herself. "There are no such things as monsters."

Realizing that she'd lagged behind the group while lost in her thoughts, she hurried to catch up. She yelped as she tripped, failing to notice a protruding root in the ground. Stumbling, she was unable to regain her footing.

Loose sediments gave way as she tottered, sending her skidding.

"Ouch!"

Brianna fell off the path, gasping as she watched herself uncontrollably race down the face of a steep ravine. "Oh god!"

Her eyes widened as a piercing howl rose up into the sky. Crying out as her head struck a rock, she quickly surrendered to black unconsciousness.

Chapter One
Waning Moon

"Drink this, Brianna, it will help warm you." The voice was dark and far away. The words were English, but the accent was thick and Russian. Brianna struggled to open her eyes, and the light that penetrated through the slit she managed sent shards of glass splintering through her mind. She felt a cup pressed to her mouth, and a warm, comforting liquid trickled down her throat.

Too soon the warm drink was taken away, and a hand came to smooth the hair away from her brow. Her body was sore, and it was difficult to use her arms and legs. It took several seconds for her to realize that it was hard to move not because of injury, but because several heavy blankets were piled upon her, weighing her down.

"You suffered a fall. You took a fever in your weak state—I have been nursing you back to health," the voice said soothingly.

"Where am I?" Her voice was raw and barely discernible.

"You're safe, Brianna."

"How do you know my name?"

A soft, masculine chuckle sounded close to her ear. "You talk in your sleep."

The hand at her brow trailed down to caress her cheek. It felt cool against her fevered skin. The covers that had imprisoned her were pushed aside, and she felt the chill of the air as it caressed her naked flesh. "You are very beautiful," he said roughly.

She tried to protest as hands palmed her breasts and plucked at her nipples, but to no avail. Her eyes would not open, her lips would not form words. She felt drugged and listless, too weak even to cry out.

Cool lips pressed softly against hers, even as she struggled for words. Sharp teeth nipped at her mouth, gentle now but with a promise of passion and danger. All the while, fingers played with her nipples, plumping them and tugging them in a way she found incredibly arousing, though it should have only made her nervous and uneasy.

Who was this man? How had he found her? She remembered the fall but then…nothing. How long had she been here with him?

She turned her head away from his kiss, but he was undeterred. His lips moved down her jaw to her neck where he brought his teeth to bear upon her. Stinging little nips at her tender skin made her gasp, and he laved the tiny hurts with his tongue. He growled softly and moved his head downward over her collarbone, biting and suckling as he went.

His hand plumped up a breast, and she felt his hot breath play over her nipple a split second before he licked her. His tongue licked a long, wet path from her nipple to her throat and onward to her lips where it speared between them to delve inside. She could not contain a moan of arousal as he masterfully kissed her.

Whoever he was, he was the sexiest kisser she'd ever locked lips with. And even though she was utterly at his mercy, she felt no fear now. She somehow sensed that this man would not bring harm to her. He seemed content to kiss and caress her, the feelings he evoked enjoyable despite her weakened, weary state.

His mouth moved down once more and latched onto a swollen nipple. She moved beneath him, no longer striving to get away, wanting only to experience more of this delicious embrace. He sucked upon her nipple, making wet noises as he feasted there. His hands were suddenly everywhere upon her, stroking her wherever he could reach.

Brianna felt his fingers slip between her thighs, and she opened her legs wider for him. Whatever madness drove him now seemed to drive her too, and she welcomed the feel of his fingertips as they parted the lips of her labia to stroke her. He unerringly found her swollen clit, and pressed it in such a way that lightning seemed to shoot straight through her.

He abruptly pulled away from her, making her gasp in disappointment. "I apologize." His voice was a low growl, his eyes penetrating. "I have restrained myself these past few days while I nursed you, but seeing you just now—awake and much recovered...I could not help myself. You will rest now—yes? You will grow strong with sleep."

With those last words Brianna felt him pull the covers back over her body. Despite the unfulfilled longing his expert touch had awakened in her, within moments she was asleep once more.

* * * * *

Ivan Davidovich Basileus looked down at his woman as she lay sleeping. Her bruises had faded to dull discolorations under her translucent skin, and the gash in her scalp was no longer swollen. Her feverish ramblings had ceased the night before, leaving her to a restful sleep at last. She was truly on the mend.

He would never forget the feeling of terror that had swamped him when he'd seen her fall down the ravine. How his heart had thudded in his chest when she'd gone limp at the rocky bottom, ending her fall in absolute stillness. He'd rushed immediately to her side, fearful of the worst.

After assuring himself that she was indeed still alive, he'd dragged her to his cabin deep within the wilderness. Here in the quiet stillness of his home, he'd seen to her scrapes and bruises with more care than he'd ever shown another living person. It was fitting, he thought, that she would inspire such protective instincts within him.

He wanted her.

He wanted to wake her, to give her no time to protest that they were strangers, and take her like a beast. This wanting of her was like a fever eating at his body and soul, one he could not fight or control. He found himself unable to leave her side for more than a few moments at a stretch, wanting only to sit in the silence and look at her face and form.

There was no way for him to rationalize or explain his fierce attraction to her. She was not a great and ravishing beauty, with her plain brown hair and brown eyes. Her skin was translucent and delicate—lending her an elfin quality, but it by no means made her the stuff of a man's wet dreams. She was thick through the bust and hips, traits that he loved on a woman—but that wasn't a good enough reason for the strength of his desire for her either.

No, her physical attributes were not what made him lust after her like an animal. This desire, this *hunger* that he had for her went far beyond such a thing. What he felt was far, far more dangerous a thing than mere physical attraction.

His cock was hard. It had been hard since the moment he first got close to her, close enough to smell the sweet floral perfume of her soap. Close enough to smell her femininity, her very femaleness. It was a heady scent, designed to drive him mad, and it succeeded very well.

He moved from the bed to a chair nearer to the fireplace across the room. Never taking his eyes from her, he sat. Unbuttoning his pants, he palmed his cock and began to stroke it. He wanted the hand pumping him to be hers, wanted it so badly that it was a physical ache, but resigned himself to wait for now.

Leaning back further in the chair, he squeezed the shaft of his erection. Massaging his balls with one hand, while stroking his penis with the other, Ivan felt his breathing quicken. Fully erect, his thick cock sported a large purple head, which soon wept a droplet of pre-cum under his hand. He swirled the liquid around, using it as lubrication while he masturbated.

In his mind he imagined Brianna moving over him, her short dark hair a halo around her head. Imagined her moaning and sheathing him in her wet pussy, over and over as she rode him. He growled softly and increased the tempo of his strokes. Soon his hips were jerking in rhythm with his hand, and his balls were tight with their load of sperm.

He heard a soft sigh from the bed as Brianna stirred in her sleep. That small sound from her lips was all it took. With a long, indrawn hiss to prevent his roar of release, he poured himself into his hand. It was several moments before he'd calmed again.

He vowed that the next time he spent himself, it would be deep within Brianna.

Chapter Two
New Moon

"So I'm stuck here until when exactly?"

"Until the snow has cleared along the trails. A few weeks at most. Are you bored with me already, Bri?"

"You know I'm not," she laughed and punched at his muscular shoulder. *Is he losing weight?* she wondered. He'd seemed so much larger those first few days after her illness. Losing weight or not he was certainly striking with his shaggy black hair and vibrant green eyes. She'd never seen a more handsome man. "But you might be getting tired of having me around all the time. You can't be used to having someone underfoot out here in the middle of nowhere."

"I could never grow tired of your company, no matter how underfoot you are." His words were teasing and light, but his eyes were dark with deeper passions. Predatory eyes feasted on her, swallowing her whole.

In the week since her recovery Brianna had stayed with Ivan, waiting for the early and unexpected snowstorm to spend itself. There were no phones or electricity here, and though Ivan had said he lived only a few hectares from a nearby village, they were essentially cut off from the outside world. At least until the snow melted away from the trails a bit.

They'd enjoyed an easy and fast friendship, and neither of them ever mentioned the stolen kisses and caresses between them that first night. Sometimes Brianna wondered if it had all been some passionate dream and could almost let herself believe it. Until moments like this, when Ivan's emerald eyes would heat and almost glow with suppressed hunger. Then she would remember every kiss, every touch and shudder with renewed desire.

She very much liked this man before her. He could be kind and gentle, as well as funny and thoughtful. Ivan was a mystery to her in many ways, but even after so short a time with him she felt as if she'd known him her whole life. He made her laugh, made her think, and never asked for anything in return but her friendship.

Ivan had saved her life, and she was very glad that he had. Otherwise she might never have met him.

But sometimes...

He made her uneasy. Like the way he could sit still for hours on end, barely blinking. He'd watched her that way, those last days when she'd been bedridden. Excusing his watchful stare by reminding herself that he was a true wilderness man—cut off from civilized society and unused to other people—she'd tried to get used to it.

The way he moved sometimes unsettled her more than when he was still. His muscles were so fluid that he moved with an almost inhuman grace at times. And he was fast. Sometimes she couldn't even see his movements. At such times, she would again remind herself of his rugged lifestyle, one that surely made him stronger and faster through strenuous labor. These reminders helped her ignore any disquiet she felt when he seemed a little...odd.

At the moment he was staring at her so intently that she almost forgot what they were talking about. Suddenly she wanted to know more about him than their friendly chitchat had revealed.

She cleared her throat. "Do you have any family nearby?"

"Yes. I have much family in the nearby village," he said, his eyes never faltering from her face. "What about you? Where is your family?"

"Oh, I don't have any. Uncle Alexi was the last of my relatives."

"Ah, yes, the one you told me about." His accent was thick and played over her like a physical caress. "The uncle who says to you, 'go—see the motherland, then fall down on your head and cause poor Ivan to have a heart attack when he finds you all bruised in a ravine'—that Uncle Alexi?"

Brianna laughed, "Yes, *that* Uncle Alexi. I was going to come later in the year when it was warmer, but I made a promise to come and I wanted to do it as soon as I could."

His eyes seemed to gentle a bit. "You wanted to get away. From his death and from your loneliness—yes?"

She looked away. "Yes. How could you tell?" She glanced back, unaccountably curious as to his response.

Ivan shrugged, firm muscles playing under his shirt. "I can see it in your eyes, this loneliness. You loved your Uncle Alexi, and now that he is gone you have no family left. You are alone now."

Brianna's eyes fell, and she looked at the hands clenched in her lap. "Yes," she quietly agreed.

"And so you come here to forget your worries for a time. It is a good thing," he said softly, his dark accent a murmur.

She smiled. "And I got to meet a new friend—that's a good thing too," she added.

He stilled. His emerald eyes bore into hers. "Yes. That's a very good thing."

*　*　*　*　*

Later, they gathered firewood for the long evening ahead. Brianna's heavy coat—borrowed from Ivan's closet—covered her from head to foot, but the wind was still cold and biting. When she'd fallen down the ravine, her backpack had contained two changes of clothing, though none of the articles were warm enough for this snowy weather. She was glad he was such a large man, and that his coat kept most of the wind at bay.

"Where do you get your kindling? Isn't this forest protected because of its age?"

Ivan growled, "Not this part of the forest. The government has no desire to save all of the Old Forest. They only conserve the areas that are home to endangered species."

"But most of these trees are hundreds, even thousands of years old. You and those villagers don't cut them down for firewood do you?" Her voice was appalled. She and her uncle had spent their whole lives trying to prevent such things with their conservation efforts.

"No! I use the younger trees, the saplings and diseased wood. I am not a butcher to take the lives of the great trees." He sliced his hand through the air, a wholly passionate and Russian expression. "Such a thing would be a crime in every way. These trees cannot be replaced, not for lifetimes, and the creatures that live here deserve the shelter of the living forest."

There was a moment of silence. "I'm sorry I doubted you." She smiled and threw a snowball at his head.

Ivan sputtered as the snowball made contact. With a growl he tossed down the armload of kindling he'd gathered and reached to make a snowball of his own. Brianna laughed and turned to run, slipping on the loose snow.

After only two steps Ivan tackled her. She felt like she'd been hit by a freight train as she stumbled to the ground.

Sputtering around a mouthful of snow she looked up into his deep, forest eyes. "Why did you do that? I thought we were having a snowball fight, not playing football!"

He cocked his head to the side, an endearing trait she'd noticed he affected when he was playful or curious. "But you ran."

"Of course I ran, you big jerk—I'm not going to just stand still and wait for your snowball to hit me!"

"I thought you ran because you wanted me to chase you. Do you not like to play chase?"

"Well, I—I don't think I've every really thought about it." What an odd question. She was suddenly very aware of his weight pressing down on her in the snow. His warm breath played over her face, and she found herself surprised by the long length of his black eyelashes.

"Well I do...so long as I catch my prey." With those words still sounding on the air between them, he swooped down and kissed her.

It was the first intimate touch between them since the night she'd awakened from her fever. Remembering and dreaming of those first kisses had consumed her every waking thought and the reality was even better. He tasted like wild forest air and dark desire.

The kiss grew heated and impassioned. Their breaths shuddered into each other's mouths as their tongues dueled in a dance as old as time. Ivan's hair tickled her face, its softness like that of an exotic fur.

The snow and cold were forgotten as Brianna's arms came around him to hold him closer. Ivan's hips ground against hers. He growled into her mouth—an animalistic sound of need.

Pulling away from her, he looked deep into her eyes— that sudden stillness he possessed coming over him. Several heartbeats passed as they panted into each other's face, breath steaming the air between them.

"I want you." His voice was a guttural growl.

"I—I want you too," she admitted.

"Then I will take you." His eyes glowed with the words, and he flew to his feet with her already secured in his arms.

He was very, very strong. She wasn't a featherweight, but he bore her as though she were. It made her heart race with excitement. Swift and sure he carried her through the door of his log home, slamming the door shut with his foot, never pausing until they reached his bedroom. With gentle care he set her upon her feet before the bed.

"We should get these wet clothes off," he whispered, fighting to control his urge to roar his triumph into the night. She would soon be his. Only his.

Agreeing wholeheartedly, she rushed to remove her coat, gloves and boots. Her hands shook with her eagerness, and she felt as giddy as a virgin. She heard a rending sound and looked up to see Ivan tearing at his clothes with the same eager abandon.

Her fingers moved to unbutton her flannel shirt, but his hands were suddenly there to stop her. Her eyes rose to meet his, which were glowing so bright it was almost alarming.

"Let me do that," he said.

"Yes," she breathed.

With aching slowness he undressed her. With hands so tender and gentle that she barely felt their touch, he reverently caressed each new patch of skin as it was unveiled. It was like being seduced by butterflies—his soft and coaxing caresses playing over her skin like silken wings. She could see the hungry desire in his eyes and knew he was exerting great control over his passions to remain gentle with her.

As he uncovered her breasts he went down on his knees before her and slowly, oh so slowly, moved his mouth to press a kiss against her nipple. He gathered her to him and buried his face between the pillows of her breasts and inhaled deeply. His instincts were at war within him, and his control slipped a notch as he fell upon her with renewed fervor.

He plumped and squeezed her breasts in his hands and moved to slurp a pouting nipple into his mouth. His tongue and teeth caressed her before he widened his mouth and took in as much of her as he could. He suckled against her with a dark and endless hunger. Releasing her with an audible pop, at the last bringing his teeth scraping over her nipple, he drew a ragged moan from her parted lips. He then moved to the other breast and gave it the same attention.

Ivan looked up from the breast that he suckled to see Brianna's head flung back, breath shuddering from her parted lips. She tasted sweet and succulent, and he resisted the sudden urge to bite her — to brand her for his own. He wanted to imprint himself upon her, so that she could never see herself in the mirror without seeing him as well. It was a primal thing, a temptation he had to fight against for fear of scaring her away.

With unsteady hands he unfastened her pants, lowering them with infinite care down over her hips and thighs. Her hands rested on his shoulders to brace her as she stepped from her clothing. She stood before him nude now, as he'd imagined her so many times in the past nights.

He leaned forward and pressed a soft kiss against the soft swell of her tummy, unable to resist the urge to nip at her tender flesh with his teeth. Her breathing hitched, and he could hear her heart pounding in her chest. Drawing her scent deep within him, he lifted one of her legs up over his shoulder — careful to steady her when she faltered.

Brianna's hands speared into his hair, and her eyes lowered to meet his. She knew what he wanted to do, but no man had ever offered to do such a thing for her. His eyes were so green they swamped her vision, making her tremble in his arms.

"I want to taste you," he said in his dark, sexy voice. It played over her like a black brush of velvet. Interpreting her moans and sighs as permission, he parted her with his fingers and licked her. His tongue roved from her opening to her clit where he lingered to press and flick against her.

He licked her over and over, pausing only to suckle the flesh of her labia and clit. He lingered at her clit with heated kisses and licks, his lips, teeth, and tongue driving her wild. She moaned and writhed, but his hands were strong and kept her standing against his hungry mouth. Wet, slurping sounds filled the room, fueling their desire, urging them on. Ivan moaned against her, the vibrations playing along her like an earthquake.

Her vaginal walls clenched, and he seemed to sense it. He speared his sinfully long tongue deep into her moist opening and thrust it into her like a cock. In and out his tongue fucked her, and his fingers came into play at her swollen, throbbing clit. She groaned as blood rushed to her cunt, swelling it further and bringing her closer and closer to orgasm. "Oh god," she gasped.

It broke over her with the force of an explosion. She flushed from her cheeks to her mons, body heated to the boiling point. Her legs buckled, and she would have fallen if not for his great strength supporting her. She cried out in a high keening wail. The tremors shook her for what seemed like an eternity, her vision going dark with the force of it.

Ivan felt the tremors of her orgasm encase his tongue like a clenching fist. He knew that as long as he lived he would never forget the taste of her. The feel and scent of her—his woman.

When her orgasm had subsided to small, deep tremors, he lowered her leg and stood. He remained still for a long moment, saying nothing—only staring into her eyes unblinking. It unsettled her until she saw his shoulders tremble with the effort to keep from pouncing on her. It sent an electric thrill of anticipation zinging through her.

His eyes burned into hers, and his hands jerked her roughly against his hard body. "Taste yourself on my tongue," he growled and kissed her. It was a branding kiss, one of possession and obsession.

Without knowing how she got there, she suddenly found herself beneath him on the bed as he kissed her. His hands and mouth were everywhere—it was like being made love to by a hurricane. Her hands roved free and desperate over his body, playing over his taut muscles, lingering when he growled or sighed over a particular caress.

He thrust her legs wide, holding her ankles in his large hands. Brianna saw his cock, poised and waiting before her. For a moment she felt a thrill of excitement and surprise upon seeing the length and breadth of him. It would be a tight fit.

She watched as he positioned the great, mushroomed head against her wet flesh and gasped as it began to sink into her. It stretched and burned her, his flesh so hot, like he was slipping a branding iron into her. He filled her, taking her more completely than she'd ever been before. When he was halfway sheathed he stopped, and she moaned.

His jaw was tight, his eyes more intense than ever before. "You are mine now," he vowed.

"Don't stop," she begged, shameless.

"Say it," he demanded. "Say you are mine."

He was so earnest that she knew he would take her words as a promise. Thinking back over the past several days with him, she knew she was growing to truly love him. But could she promise herself to him? She knew that if she spoke the words there would be no going back for either of them. Ever.

"Say it," he growled again, withdrawing from her slightly, making her feel bereft and empty.

"I—I'm yours." Her voice shook.

"Say it again."

"I'm yours. I'm yours!" she vowed, feeling as though her soul were somehow threading itself to his.

"Mine," he breathed, gifting her with a sweet kiss before thrusting to the hilt inside of her.

They both groaned at the exquisite sensation. Unable to wait any longer, they began to rock back and forth against each other. Brianna brought her legs around his waist, hooking her ankles at the small of his back. He thrust in and out of her, somehow reaching deeper and deeper inside of her with every stroke.

Soon they were both sweating with their efforts, the scent of sex and lust heady in the air. They caught each other's cries with their mouths, moaning and gasping, trembling and writhing upon the bed. Ivan growled and bit sharply into her shoulder, teeth securing her beneath him as he thrust ever more fiercely into her. Brianna gasped at the pain, but it drove her passion up to a fevered pitch.

They came together, Brianna's body bucking beneath him, screaming in her wild ecstasy. Ivan's body went taut inside of hers as he threw back his head on a booming roar. Her body milked his of its seed, her pussy squeezing like a greedy mouth on his cock.

Ivan collapsed on her, his weight crushing her into the bed. She welcomed it, clutching him to her as her heart slowed. Their heavy breathing echoed through the room, slowly quieting until Brianna drifted off to sleep.

Before her dreams could take her she heard a howl in the night and Ivan whispering the words, "The moon is growing."

Chapter Three
Waxing Moon – one week later

A voice spoke at her ear; "I want you again. Now."

Brianna roused from her exhausted sleep as she felt Ivan's thick cock probe at her from behind.

"We did it four times last night, Ivan. I'm tired," she protested, even as her body awakened to the passion his appetite inspired within her.

His teeth bit into the tender flesh between her neck and shoulder. He seemed to enjoy biting her, and she certainly liked it too. She grew damp, and then wet, as he raised her leg and brought it back over his hips. This opened her more fully to him, and the head of his cock slipped into her.

"You can rest later. I need you *now*." His words were harsh as he fought for control. He knew she was likely tender from their loving the night before, but his control was slipping more and more around her, and he couldn't hold himself back.

For the past week they'd spent their days and nights in each other's arms. They'd explored their deepest and darkest desires and fed on one another like gluttons. Whenever she was near, his cock would grow hard as marble and his heart would race. He knew it was the same for her, that she was just as hungry for him. Her dark eyes would flare and heat whenever he was near.

When they weren't making love they were spending their time talking and learning about each other. The more Ivan learned about Brianna the more he grew to love her. *Love* — it was too pale a description for the emotion he felt for her. She cared about the same things he did, she liked the same music and shared many of the same hobbies. She was intelligent, kind, and passionate. She was his mate, the woman of his dreams. His match in every way.

He found it difficult sometimes to share with her all the secrets he had guarded during his life. But slowly he was revealing them to her, preparing her for the knowledge he knew she must be given — must accept — for them to be truly mated. There wasn't much more time to coax her into belief or acceptance, but he was trying with each new revelation shared between them.

He wasn't like other men. He hoped she could accept it, and grow to love him because of it — not in spite of it.

Feeling her wet heat surround the head of his cock, he thrust into her, resting against the mouth of her womb. He tried to calm his breathing, to cool his ardor, but it was useless. She was too much of a temptation, and he was soon thrusting in and out of her with firm strokes.

"Am I hurting you, my little one?" he asked in a thick Russian accent. He breathed a sigh of relief when she assured him he wasn't. She moaned beneath him, and he couldn't hold back a growl of satisfaction. He licked his thumb and forefinger, using the wetness on her nipple, which grew hard like a diamond under his attention.

He thrust into her, feeling her flooding wetness soaking them both. Knowing he was close to his orgasm, his hand moved from her nipple. He moved his hand lower, and found her swollen clit, massaging in the way he knew she liked best. He felt the first, faint tremors of her climax and let loose of his iron control.

Brianna's body felt swollen with her passion and need. No matter how often or how thoroughly they loved, it felt altogether new and exciting every time. She moaned as his hand roved over her with a masterful touch. He played her like an instrument, knowing just when to press and when to retreat to make her nerves sing with pleasure.

His cock filled and stretched her. In the last few days, she'd felt empty and bereft if he wasn't inside her. Her body felt like a separate and self-serving thing, content only when they were in each other's arms. She couldn't deny him anything. It was as frightening as it was magical.

As his fingers plucked and massaged her clit, she came, clamping like a vice down upon his cock as he pumped his seed into her. Ivan cried out, a broken, ragged sound that thrilled her even as she cried out in unison.

After a few moments their breathing had calmed. "Go back to sleep, Bri. I'll make us some breakfast," he said with a kiss to her ear. She felt him rise from the bed and was struck with an idea.

"It's not more venison is it? I don't think my stomach can take much more venison—no matter how you prepare it," she said with a smile, thinking back to all the different dishes he'd concocted with venison being the main ingredient.

He smiled back. "How about wild hare then?"

"Why all the meat? Why not eggs or cereal? Hell, I'd eat oatmeal—and I hate oatmeal," she laughed.

"Eggs will not keep very long, and I can't have any chickens about. There are wolves, in case you weren't aware." His grin was positively feral. "Besides, this is the best time of the month for hunting, right before the full moon."

"Yuck. You know you talk like a woman with PMS, mentioning the phases of the moon and junk all the time," she laughed, but he remained oddly still and silent. She ignored it, not liking the niggling suspicion that if she probed too deep she would be opening the proverbial Pandora's box. "Why don't you surprise me then," she asked with a grin.

"I think I can manage that," he said with a grin of his own, and donning a thick robe he left for the kitchen. With a laugh and a girlish squeal she burrowed beneath the covers.

* * * * *

"The moon is growing," he whispered. If she hadn't been nestled in his arms at the window she wouldn't have heard him.

"You know, you must be a closet astronomer," she teased. "You've said that before."

He merely grunted, his chest vibrating under her ear, and she snuggled deeper in his embrace. He'd gained back the flesh that he'd lost, his muscles firm and bulging beneath her, making her feel safe and loved.

"It's so bright," he said in a singsong voice. He was wound tight beneath her; she could almost feel the contained energy pouring off of him in waves.

"It will be a full moon in a couple of days," she agreed, worried for reasons she couldn't fathom.

"A full moon." He lingered over the last word so that it sounded like '*moooooon*'.

A single howl ruptured the quiet of the night. She shivered.

Ivan's hand tilted her face up into the moonlight. He'd gone still in that odd way of his, emerald eyes boring into hers. She could see his pupils widening and closing over and over, like a telescope lens. His eyes were alight with a strange inner fire.

He breathed deeply, as if drawing her scent deep into his lungs. Nostrils flaring, eyes flashing, he seemed more animal than man. It unnerved her, but despite that her heart raced with excitement. Ivan was the most dangerous and attractive man she'd ever met, and she loved him. He thrilled her, moved her. She couldn't imagine how she'd ever lived without him in her life.

She wanted him. Suddenly, desperately, she had to have him.

Leaning forward she pressed her lips to his, hearing him make a sound like a whimper before he crushed her to him. He grew wild, tearing at her clothes and growling with the same desperate hunger she felt. With amazing strength he lifted them both from the chair on which they'd been cuddled to bring her before the window.

He turned her from him, coming behind her and quickly removing the rest of her clothing. She stood there beneath the light of the moon, feeling a bestial lust overtake her. Ivan bit her neck, and she moaned. With rough hands he pulled her back against him, and she felt his naked flesh press tightly to hers.

Their skin grew heated, his burning at her back like a roaring fire. He bent her forward and thrust fully into her, balls slapping against her as he slid home.

"Be gentle," she urged as she felt herself stretched to the fullest. He was so very large tonight, larger than she'd ever known him to be.

"I cannot," he said raggedly. His voice was guttural and rough. "Not now. Tell me if I hurt you, Bri." Moaning, he slammed into her.

She gasped. Not in pain, as she'd expected, but in overwhelming ecstasy. Her pussy was filled with his cock, and the angle at which he penetrated her brought him in direct contact with all the secret, pleasurable places deep inside of her.

Pleasure and pain blurred, his hands, mouth and teeth were everywhere they could reach, his cock so deep inside of her she felt split in two. A keening, animalistic noise sounded over and over, and Brianna realized the sound was spilling from her own lips.

"*Ooooh, Ooooooh,* God yes! Don't stop!" she cried out over and over.

"Who owns you, heart and soul? Whom do you belong to?" he demanded.

"You, I belong to you. Only you!" she vowed, in between short, high screams.

Their bodies slapped audibly, sweat covering them in a fine sheen. "Come for me," he commanded. "Come for me now."

She did. Immediately upon hearing his words her pussy clenched like a fist around him and he pounded even more furiously into her. She started wailing, nearly screaming as her body pulsed and trembled. The orgasm was explosive, intense and consuming.

When she'd calmed she realized Ivan was far from through with her. He went down on his knees before her and buried his mouth against her. He licked and sucked and tongue-fucked her until she came again.

Legs trembling, mindless after the violence of her orgasms, all Brianna could do was moan and thrash against him as he lay on the floor, seating her on top of him. His thick shaft filled her to the hilt, reaching her womb.

"Ride me," he growled.

With his hands lending her strength, she rode him, moving upon him eagerly. Unbelievably he grew wilder as she undulated over him. His face tilted up towards the moon, eyes flashing on hers in the silver illumination. His teeth flashed, looking sharp and strange behind his sensuous lips. He moaned and groaned beneath her, hips bucking against her, hands clutching against the flesh of her hips.

He grew suddenly taut beneath her, head thrown back. Brianna's orgasm shook through her a scant second before his sperm flooded through her. Ivan thrashed beneath her and howled a long cry into the moonlit night.

Brianna collapsed on him, limp without his support, and heard him vow into her ear, "You will never leave me. Not now, not ever."

Chapter Four
Full Moon

Ivan was acting strange. Even more than what was usual for him. His hair was wild and unkempt, his eyes sharp and darting. Brianna had only known him for a month, but in that time she'd learned enough about him to be concerned about his behavior. She could see he was in some kind of distress, but when she asked him what was wrong he only barked at her and retreated outdoors.

He left her for hours at a time, coming back looking wild and dangerous. He would immediately take her body like a beast, mercilessly slamming in and out of her cunt for hours on end.

The attraction between them was very strong, but because of his odd behavior in the past few days she was starting to feel, well...*nervous.*

Sex with him was wild and untamed. She'd had so many orgasms she'd lost count, and Ivan never seemed to tire of wringing them from her. He'd fucked her in every orifice—her cunt, her mouth, even her ass—a place she'd never been touched before—and still he'd wanted more and more of her.

In the past two days they'd barely spoken. They'd been too busy screwing each other's brains out. Brianna loved him and was certain that he was growing to love her too. But she worried about what inner torment he was going through.

But when she tried to draw him out of his shell, he'd shut her out completely. Perhaps it was just a mood, but he seemed so distant from her unless they were making love. Shuttered and withdrawn.

"The moon is full tonight," he spoke, breaking into her thoughts. He stood in the doorway apparently having just arrived from one of his walks.

"Really?" She tried to sound interested. He talked about the moon a lot.

"We must talk." His voice was serious and firm. Her heart sank, as she feared that he'd grown tired of her already and was trying to find a way to break things off with her. She tried not to let her sadness show.

"Okay," she said, surprised that her voice sounded so neutral and steady.

"There are things about me you must know. About me and my family…and the people of the village. Things you won't understand…but I need you to try."

"You're scaring me," she whispered.

"I am sorry. I wish I could give you more time, but the moon…" He faltered, and for the first time Brianna saw that he was nervous and unsure of himself.

"Hey, it's all right. You can tell me," she coaxed, taking his hands in hers.

He sighed. "I am not like other men, Brianna. My family and the inhabitants of the nearby village are not like normal people. We are very different." He was quiet for a moment. She could almost hear the gears turning in his head. "To put it bluntly, we are not human."

"W—*what*?" She tried to laugh his proclamation off, but couldn't seem to summon even a threadbare chuckle. Her throat was dry, the word sounding hoarse and faint even to her own ears. His revelation was worse than she'd expected.

He was mad.

"What do you mean by that exactly?" Her voice hardened on the last words.

"Do not withdraw from me." His voice caught as he reached for her when she would have pulled away. "I could not bear it if you turned from me now. I had hoped we were growing close—close enough for this. I love you. I have loved you from the first, and it would kill me if you turned from me now."

"I love you too, Ivan. So much. But you're scaring me. You've been so distant the past few days, and when you do talk to me you sound like you're angry. I feel like you're pushing me away. And now this—you're just not making sense!"

"I am sorry, but I have no words to tell you that will make sense. I have never told anyone—never had to. I rarely meet humans, my kind tend to keep to themselves here in the forest, we always have. I am not like you, I am...*other*."

"You're talking like a crazy man," she breathed out. "And you're scaring me."

He swore in Russian, running a hand through his dark hair. "I have not the English to tell you what I am. But my kind, we are very different from yours. We go through phases, with the moon as our guide. Every full moon we change into...into wolves—not like normal wolves, but very close," he spoke over her gasp, laying a hand on her mouth to silence her until he was finished. She tried to pull away, but he secured her to him, exerting little strength in doing so.

"With the waning moon, after the change, we lose our wolfish traits, our glowing eyes dim, our fangs retreat and our bodies lose muscle mass. During the new moon we are very much like humans, though we retain some of our strength and speed. During the waxing moon the cycle begins anew, and we approach the change with heightened senses, increased muscle mass and sharper teeth.

"Then, on the full moon we change. We become like wolves, on four legs, with fur and fangs. We hunt the night as our instincts demand, thinning out the weaker prey and communing with nature." His emerald eyes were lit, intense, his jaw clenched. "We are not human."

Brianna tried again to pull away from him and this time he let her. She was shaking, not with fear of him as he suspected, but with fear for him. For his sanity. What he was telling her was impossible.

"You're not a werewolf. Your family and those villagers are not werewolves. You're just confused—but we can get you some help." Tears choked her as her mind raced. He needed doctors, the best that money could buy. Luckily she had enough money to get him the treatment he needed. "I promise I'll help you get well."

"You don't understand, but you will. The night is upon us, and the moon is on the rise. You will see the truth of my words then. Just know that I am sorry I cannot help you through this. I would give you more time to know me before you see what I am, but it is impossible."

"If you're what you say you are, then why pick me? Why not pick one of your own kind to…to love?" She faltered. She loved him so much that she was starting, in some dark corner of her mind, to believe him a little.

"I don't know, and I have never before heard of an interspecies mating. I'm not even sure we can produce offspring, you and I, though I want to try. We mate for life," he said firmly. "We mate for life, instinctively knowing when we've found the right one. You're my one, my woman, and my mate. And whether or not you believe me, I will love you forever, even if you turn from me in horror after tonight. I am still yours."

"Have you never...mated before me?" she whispered.

"You are the only woman I've ever lain with. The only woman I've ever wanted to lie with. Before you there was only my hand and my fantasies of a faceless mate — you. I will never lie with another. *There is only you*," he vowed.

"I first saw you when you entered the forest," he continued. "You captivated me, pulled at me and lured me. I followed you, sometimes as a wolf because of the full moon, and sometimes as a man, but I could not let you out of my sight. You haunted me. When I saw you fall down that ravine, I almost died of fright. You have no idea how thankful I was when I realized you were alive."

Her eyes were rounded. "How can that be? It's just not possible. I'm scared for you, Ivan. I love you, but this..." She trailed off as she became aware of the gathering darkness. Ivan's eyes glowed, like emeralds in the shadows.

"You can watch me change." His voice was rough and guttural. "I will leave afterwards, to hunt with my pack, but I will be back at dawn. If you find that you do not want to see me again, leave the front door closed and locked and I will go. I will send someone to fetch you and take you away from here. I will let you go, but I will miss you." His voice broke, sadness permeating every word. "I love you," he murmured.

He backed out of the house, out into the snow. Brianna helplessly followed, openly weeping. He was so earnest, she wanted to believe him—anything to know his mind wasn't deranged.

The rising moon illuminated him as he removed his clothing. Brianna protested, trying to stop him, but was interrupted as a howl rose from his lips. Brianna gasped as she saw Ivan fall to the ground writhing. She rushed to his side.

"Get away," he growled and turned his head up to the moon. What she saw nearly stopped her heart. His face was changing. His teeth had sharpened and elongated, and the bones of his face seemed to be shifting beneath the skin. "Go back to the house, Bri. I might hurt you in the other form—" He howled again, his entire body beginning to shift.

Brianna raced back to the house as he'd instructed, knowing her presence wasn't needed. She watched from the window as her lover shifted into a wolf. As the change progressed, she saw that he was much larger than any ordinary wolf, and far more wildly beautiful. His fur was black and thick, shining in the moonlight. He was stout and heavily muscled, with powerful jaws and gleaming fangs.

Never in her wildest dreams would she have thought it possible—a man actually shape-shifting. At first she was afraid, afraid of him and for him. But after watching his body shift and change for a few moments she was reminded of the butterfly and the chrysalis, a magical transformation—and yet still earthbound and natural. Mother Nature had many secret wonders. Brianna believed her werewolf was one of them.

When the change was complete a powerful, black wolf stood before the window. The wolf looked straight at her with Ivan's bright green eyes, seeming almost sad for a moment, before he turned and ran into the forest. Brianna cried out, weeping at the raw beauty of the miracle she'd witnessed, wishing she could go with him.

Brianna spent the night listening to the distant howling and baying of wolves. Her world was forever changed. She was in love with a werewolf, mated to him. Forever bound to him. At once she realized that life with Ivan would never be dull, and she laughed through renewed tears. Though there was much to be discussed between them, Brianna was ever eager to welcome her lover back.

She was his, and he was hers. In every way…forever.

When a nude Ivan returned at dawn, the door was wide open, and she waited for him in a nightshirt on the porch steps. He smiled, positively wolfish in his relief and triumph. He rushed to sweep her up into his arms, taking her straight to bed where he came down to rest upon her.

"Do you accept me then? You're not afraid of me?" he asked, and when his lips moved Brianna could clearly see his sharpened, elongated teeth.

"I'm not afraid of you. Are you afraid of me?" Brianna teased.

He ignored her gibe. "I would understand if you were. You can't have met many people like me."

"You mean Russian people? I don't know…if ever there was a country to find them in, this would be it."

"I'm trying to be serious," but he laughed anyway.

"No, I'm not afraid of you, Ivan," her voice trailed to a whisper, and she took his face in her hands. "I want to know everything there is to know about being mated to a werewolf…I'm going to need all the help I can get." She kissed his nose.

He grinned, obviously relieved. "My mother and sister will be happy to guide you—they are eager to meet you, along with the rest of the pack. They are curious about the first human woman to join our family."

"I hope they don't think I'm not good enough for you."

"They would never think that. My instincts knew you for my mate from the start. There can be no objections to the rightness of our bonding. My heart belongs to you, and that is as it should be."

Ivan moved against her, and Brianna was suddenly reminded of his nudity. She wrapped her legs around his back, forcing a groan from him.

"I missed you last night," she whispered.

Ivan let out a small howling sound and pushed up her nightshirt with rough hands. "I'll try not to be rough, but it's hard so soon after a change."

"Be rough. I don't mind." Her words were swift with her rising excitement.

Hearing the words seemed to dissolve what little control he had left. He growled and tore her clothes from her body, making her gasp. His mouth slammed down onto hers, hungry and demanding. She felt the scrape of his teeth and brought her own to bear in the kiss.

Ivan's hands were everywhere on her, and his mouth soon followed. His hair, longer after his change, tickled over her skin as he loved her. He rolled their bodies and sat up, so that she straddled him. His cock was pressed against her wet core. He rocked her back and forth, causing an exquisite friction that made them both gasp.

Ivan buried his face in her breasts, plumping them around his face so that he could lick and suckle at them both. His teeth scraped and then bit into her tender flesh, stopping just short of breaking the skin, making her moan with heated longing. She clutched his head to her, moving on him, bathing him in her wet heat.

Pulling his head from her grasp, he threw back his head and howled. Brianna heard the wolf in his cry, the sound far from a human one, and it thrilled her. She saw his eyes glow with their strange inner fire, and felt him lift her up, positioning her over his straining cock. As she eased down over him, enveloping him in her body, his fingernails dug into the flesh of her hips and suddenly held her still.

His eyes met hers, his warm breath huffing over her face. They sat there, breathing raggedly for several heartbeats, before Ivan thrust up — pulling her down at the same time — and sheathed himself balls deep inside of her. Moments passed, as he remained still, embedded inside of her.

"I need you so much," he whispered brokenly.

Brianna was beyond words, her love for him filled her heart as fully as his cock filled and stretched her cunt. She moaned and pressed a kiss to his mouth, riding him. Slowly at first, and then more rapidly. Ivan groaned and took control of their dance, slamming into her with a force that should have bruised her but only made her hungry for more.

The bed shook with the force of their thrusts, and soon Ivan was growling over and over again, approaching his climax. Brianna deliberately tightened her inner muscles around his shaft, wringing a cry from him. His hands dug into her flesh, and he sank his teeth into her shoulder as they moved. That small pleasure-pain was enough to nudge her to the brink, and as the inner tremors of her climax began Ivan thrust up into her—far enough that she felt she could choke on the penetration.

They came together, bathing each other with their pleasure. Rocking softly against one another until their bodies were spent. Brianna felt full with his cock and with his seed, and she'd never felt more right in his arms. Somehow she knew that she was pregnant.

After what seemed like hours, though only minutes had passed, Ivan raised his head from her shoulder and smiled.

"Let's do that again."

They both laughed and proceeded to do just that.

About the author:

Sherri L. King lives in the American Deep South with her husband, artist and illustrator Darrell King. Critically acclaimed author of The Horde Wars and Moon Lust series, her primary interests lie in the world of action packed paranormals, though she's been known to dabble in several other genres as time permits.

Sherri welcomes mail from readers. You can write to her c/o Ellora's Cave Publishing at 1337 Commerce Drive, Suite 13, Stow OH 44224.

Also by Sherri L. King:

LUNEWULF: PACK LAW

Lorie O'Clare

Prologue

"I've got the list!"

Sophia Rousseau jumped off the couch and hurried over to her older sister. Gertrude barely had a chance to take off her coat before Sophie grabbed the stapled sheets of paper from her sister's hand.

"I don't know why you are so excited to read that bitch's list." Elsa, Sophie's younger sister, appeared in the doorway. "She's trying to control our lives by telling us who to mate with."

Sophie rolled her eyes. Elsa always put a damper on things. "Quit acting like a rebellious teenager."

Sophie returned to the couch and her sisters scrunched in on either side of her. Holding her breath, she ran her finger over her pack mate's names, searching for her own.

"Oh my God." She stared at the three werewolves who Grandmother Rousseau, their pack leader, had determined would be her mates. She mouthed the three names quietly to herself: Niklas Alexander, Lukas Kade, and Jonathan Abram. For a moment, she forgot to breathe.

"You fucking scored," Gertrude whispered, grabbing the sheets to look for her own name.

Sophie stood up and walked over to the large window that looked out over the sprawling front yard. The urge to change crawled through her system, the desire to experience her emotions in their rawest forms. Her bones ached to grow stronger, stretch; a tickle began at the back of her neck, tiny hairs itching to grow, and transform her into the beautiful beast that waited within.

"I wonder if Nik already knows." She stared out the window. An image of his penetrating blue eyes appeared before her, eyes that always watched her, judged her. And showed what he wanted to do to her. He would be her alpha male—she would see to it. She would fuck him first, and she would do it soon.

"You better learn to want all of your mates." Elsa's disapproving tone didn't faze Sophie. "We're the lucky bitches who get to breed with three wolves."

Her imitation of their grandmother made Sophie smile. In spite of her sister's views, Sophie didn't find it disgusting at all. They were lucky to have three wolves at their beck and call—especially three fine wolves like hers! She turned around and grinned at her sisters.

"Nik will be my alpha. But Jonathan and Lukas are good men too."

"You just love the idea of fucking all of them." Gertrude giggled, handing the list of names to Elsa. "I got the men that I wanted, too."

Elsa tossed the stapled sheets onto the coffee table. "I don't want any of these wolves. I don't see how you two can be so excited about being told who to fuck. Shit ladies, this is the twenty-first century, not the dark ages."

"You need to take more pride in being *lunewulf*," Gertrude told her.

"I agree." Sophie turned again to stare past the yard, the itch to run across the meadows distracting her.

The rich scent of the earth, the wonderful array of greens, with the endless deep blue sky overhead would soothe the fears she couldn't seem to overcome despite her acceptance of pack law. But it excited her too. She would have three werewolves, all different, their bodies and cocks hers to explore. She wanted to lie in the meadow, imagining them, and run her fingers in and out of her soaked pussy.

But three werewolves! Could she handle three?

Ignoring her own fears, she turned her attention back to her sister.

"Whether or not you agree with the methods the pack has decided upon, it's important to keep the *lunewulf* breed strong. We're one of the oldest breeds of werewolves in the world. And you know males outnumber females. We get three mates so that we don't die out."

"I'm not going to be shackled to three men." Elsa would get herself in trouble if she protested too loud, but Sophie was tired of arguing with her.

Not to mention, she'd rather dream about what was in store for her: Nik, with his powerful body, that sexy stroll, his cocky grin, those long muscular legs, kept her awake at night with lustful longing.

His cock was huge. He'd pressed it against her many times. Just the thought of that rock-hard penis pushing deep inside her made her tremble with need. Heat surged through her, and she licked her lips, imagining his hot come squirting while she sucked that enormous cock.

Gertrude was right. She couldn't wait to fuck!

Chapter One

The rich, thick aroma in the air couldn't be mistaken. Everyone here wanted to fuck.

In the living room, Sophie's sister Trudy gyrated to the thumping music. Pack members lingered everywhere in the small house, enjoying the party. Some werewolves from a pack south of Prince George had shown up too.

Damp air coming through the window gave her goosebumps when she passed in front of it, weaving around the people who hovered at the dining room table, munching on the snacks.

Salt, lust, sweat and bitter cigarette smoke permeated the close quarters. Her hair would stink tomorrow. Sophie tucked a blonde strand behind her ear, then leaned against the wall, next to the window, to enjoy the hint of outdoors that trickled in.

Everyone will end up in the corners fucking before the night is over, her cousin Simone had said when she came by to pick up Sophie and her sisters at their grandmother's house.

I want to get fucked tonight. She searched the room to see if *he* had arrived yet—hopefully, it wasn't obvious she didn't care about the party. Ever since she had turned eighteen, *he* had consumed her thoughts. Nik always seemed to be nearby, but she had it on good authority from Simone, that he planned to be at Johann's party.

I'm wherever you are because I am watching you. Nik had stood behind her at the last pack meeting and whispered in her ear. *You are mine. Our dens have chosen you for me, and I plan to make my mark very soon.*

His wicked promise had kept her on the verge of an orgasm for the past week. Her throbbing clit drove her to distraction. Now, thick cream saturated her panties just thinking about what he'd said. The October breeze seeping through the window did nothing to ease the intense heat of her aching pussy.

"Elsa, wait for me." Sophie's sister left the kitchen, heading for the back door. "I'll go outside with you." Maybe Nik would be outside.

"You aren't having any fun either?" Elsa shoved her long blonde hair over her shoulder. Worry clouded her pretty blue eyes.

Sophie ran her hand over her baby sister's hair. "It's a bit warm in here. But you should relax. You'd have more fun. There are tons of sexy wolves here tonight."

Elsa looked even more troubled, but Sophie couldn't help smiling. Her sister acted like a prude. How could they be from the same den?

When she followed Elsa out the back door, the cold night air slapped her face. A large group circled a bonfire in the corner of the yard. Sophie stepped around her sister to look for Nik.

Her heart pounded faster and blood raced through her veins; the primal urge to change filled her being. The beast in her, the beautiful *lunewulf*, begged to be released. Wood-smoke mixed with the crisp sweetness of the pines growing on the edge of the property. The night air wrapped around her, drawing her nipples to hardened peaks. She loved the cold, the change of autumn to winter. It made her frisky, full of life and the desire to run and play. Rolling in the meadows with a certain tall, well-built *lunewulf* would make the night perfect.

She wandered into the yard toward the bonfire. But the partiers didn't impress her. At the other end, over by the group of parked cars, deep, male baritones grabbed her attention, heightening her lust-torn nerves. Could Nik be with that group?

She glanced back at Elsa. Johann had found her. Good. Her sister would be distracted. Sophie put a strut in her walk, and strolled across the yard. A beer might calm her nerves.

"Looking good, Sophie." Lukas Kade grinned from the other side of the keg, while holding the black tube that pumped beer into a plastic cup. He handed the cup to her, spilling the golden brew over the edges.

"Thanks, Lukas." Sophie never knew what to say to the stocky man.

She sipped at the beer and watched over the rim as Lukas approached her. He grabbed her shoulder, his thick fingers squeezing her bones, then leaned in to bury his head in her hair.

"I love your scent. I can almost taste the rich cream from your pussy when I'm near you. We need to get together soon." Thick fingers rubbed against her tummy then moved under her sweater to cup her breast. Calloused roughness brushed her hardened nipple. Electric tingles shot through her, and a nervous sweat broke out over her chilled skin.

Sawdust, beer, and lust consumed her senses when she inhaled the air around Lukas. She molded into him, his powerful body wrapping around hers like a warm blanket. Of her three mates, he would be her teddy bear.

"I can't wait to feel that hot little mouth of yours around my cock," he whispered, the pungent beer on his breath saturating the air. Lukas kneaded her breast, sending nervous energy flaring through her.

They were practically strangers, since he'd graduated several years ahead of her. But he was a good wolf, raised in a hardworking den.

Will I grow to love you, too?

Hands fondled her ass. Slow caresses robbed her of her rational thought, long fingers stroking downward toward her steamy cunt.

Abruptly her head cleared. When she opened her eyes, Lukas held her head in one hand; his other fingers squeezed her breast hard enough to make his mark. But someone else now stood behind her. Someone with experienced fingers that seemed to know right where to press through her jeans, causing her silk panties to dance around her swollen clit.

She couldn't think. Sensations rippled through her. Pressure built deep in her womb; her cunt pulsed with anticipation. Skilled fingers pressed and rubbed, fire plunging through her that she couldn't stop. Didn't want to stop. The world around her blurred, and she exploded, coming hard.

She bit her lip so she wouldn't cry out...and turned her head to see who had brought her to a complete orgasm in her cousin's backyard during the middle of a party.

Chapter Two

Eyes dark with lust stared down at her. Relief and excitement swept Sophie.

Nik stood behind her, his hand still stoking the feverish heat in her pussy. Her legs turned to putty when she met Nik's darkly satisfied gaze.

"Damn Sophie, you just came." Lukas tried to pull her to him, but Nik clamped an arm around her waist, pinning her.

"Looks like you've had plenty to drink tonight, Kade." Nik's rich baritone sent shivers through Sophie.

Nik took a step backward, forcing Lukas' hand out from under her sweater. Lukas' gaze clouded. He gathered his bearing before looking over her shoulder at Nik.

"You can't hog her to yourself." Lukas' voice sounded gravelly. Extended teeth pressed over his lower lip and glossy white fur covered his cheeks. "She's my mate too."

Sophie could hardly focus on anything other than the powerful arms around her. Nik had a body of steel; hard, firm muscles offered a wall of strength. The throbbing steel length of Nik's cock burned into her lower back. Her insides swarmed with heat. Fire nestled inside the folds of her pussy. Raw, untamed sex filled the air around them. Though she'd barely quit shaking from coming, already she wanted Nik's cock.

"We've talked about this, Kade. We decided how to do it." Nik let her go, and the cold night air swooped in, chilling her.

You talked about what? Sophie looked at Nik, then back at Lukas. "What have you decided to do?"

Lukas' grin turned as mischievous as a schoolboy's. But Nik pulled her away from her other mate and across the yard.

"What did you talk about?"

They moved through the parked cars, where several of her pack mates noticed her being led by the arm and grinned.

Nik let go of her, but his touch remained branded on her skin. Tall meadow grass tangled around her thighs. She stomped through it, following him toward the thick line of pines that bordered the property.

"You're nervous about mating with all three of us." Nik turned to face her and crossed his arms over his chest.

His statement rendered her silent for a moment. All her fears surfacing, she stared at him. Straw-blond hair framed his face—a beautiful face with high cheekbones and deep blue eyes that watched her like a hawk does its prey.

"Don't tell me how I'm thinking, wolf man." Some of the bitches, like Elsa, had rebelled against pack decision to have polygamous mating. But Nik and most of his den were politically active within the pack. Sophie wouldn't be known as a rebel. "I can't wait to have the three of you at my beck and call."

"You will come to each of us when we howl for you and fuck us with pleasure?" His gaze penetrated her, seemingly able to pinpoint each of her fears. But standing here, with Nik Alexander inches from her, fogged her senses. Her ass still tingled from where his cock had pressed against her. The burning need inside her grew too powerful to restrain.

I will fuck you with pleasure any time, wolf man.

"Well of course." She dared to take a step toward him, keeping her gaze locked with his. "I believe in keeping the *lunewulf* breed intact and whole. Pack law states a bitch should provide cubs for three different werewolves. I don't break laws."

"And you aren't scared?"

She reached out to him. Her fingertips charged with the heat from his body the moment she pressed them against his rock-hard chest.

"No," she lied, brushing her fingers over his soft sweatshirt. Fire burned in Nik's beautiful blue eyes.

"I don't frighten you?" He reached out to touch her cheek, and swept aside a strand of her hair.

Sophie swallowed. She would offer him some honesty, before her buried fears filled the air with their stench. Nik had been the man of her dreams throughout high school, her protector when the older werewolves picked on her. Now that she'd turned twenty and was old enough to breed, he would be her mate, and he stood before her demanding to know her feelings.

She whispered the first thing that came to mind. "I want you." Her cheeks burned with her embarrassment.

He studied her, appearing to understand her feelings better than she. The night air chilled her lungs; a yearning to change and run through the trees behind him overtook her, heightening her emotions, intensifying her desires.

Running would ruin the moment. *That* she wouldn't allow. And she sure as hell wouldn't say anything else to embarrass herself. Straightening, she stuck out her chin and waited for his response.

"Take off your clothes." His expression didn't change, but his blue eyes sparked with lust. Their fire caught deep in her gut, swelling and smoldering.

"What?" She gasped, her heart pounding loud enough to make it hard to hear.

"You stand before me showing your boldness. Without fear." He dropped his hand so that his fingers rubbed her oversensitive nipples. Sparks ignited in her, quickening in her womb.

Her cardigan abraded her nipples, he squeezed, torturing them into eager hardness. "You like your nipples pinched, don't you, my little bitch?"

She moaned, unwilling to admit the quick sensation of pain could cause the rush of cream that drenched her panties.

"I want my mate naked before me," he growled. His mouth changed shape as his teeth grew. His request aroused him; the change rippling through him proved that.

He wanted her as badly as she wanted him.

Come dripped from her throbbing pussy lips; her insides tightened with nervous lustful energy. *He is challenging me, testing my boldness. And if I told him I had fears, he would soothe them for me.*

But did she want tender? Sophie managed a smile, although her lips quivered from the cold and the emotions that flooded her. She grabbed the bottom of her sweater, pulled it over her head before she chickened out.

She boiled inside and her heart pounded ruthlessly in her chest. The night air's icy fingers traced over her feverish skin, making her breath come in quick gasps. Dropping her sweater, she knelt in front of him to undo her boot laces.

"You are beautiful, Sophie, so beautiful."

Though she couldn't see his face, she could watch his hand move on his cock. Her fingers fumbled the laces while he stroked himself, his small movements proving an almost unbearable distraction.

"I'm cold. I want to change." Her bones popped in agony, and she couldn't help murmuring her desire even though she wanted him to see her as a confident bitch.

"Fight it. I want to see you in your flesh." He rubbed the thick, growing bulge in his pants.

She stood and slipped out of her jeans and panties, dropping her clothes in a pile next to her. Then she faced him, naked and on fire, in spite of the biting night air — it only added to the torturous flames that burned in her pussy. Frigid air embraced her feverish cunt. Icy fire teased her clit; it ached with cold, with heat, with anticipation.

"Look at you." He pulled her into his arms, wrapping her in the heat of his body, his strength feeding her. "You are mine, Sophie. I'll share you with your other two mates, but, my sweet little *lunewulf* bitch, you are mine."

Chapter Three

There had been other bitches, willing women in his pack who would spread their legs in a meadow. Some of them had been quite good, but none of them had been Sophie. He'd watched her throughout high school, and then afterwards, with her sisters at pack meetings, or around town and at parties.

He knew years ago he would make her his bitch, the mother of his cubs. And maybe he'd expressed that interest to the right people when decisions were made about who would be mated with whom. He would share her, but only under his terms.

Nik lifted Sophie into his arms, her smooth skin torturing him worse than he thought possible. He couldn't believe her boldness, not to mention her eagerness to do as he said. Her submission made his cock burn with the need to be inside her. He wanted her cunt, her sweet mouth and her tight ass. He wanted her to know that she belonged to *him* first.

I might have to share her cunt, but no one else will fuck her ass. He would hear her swear to that.

He trusted Sophie, but her word was not enough. He needed the word of her other two mates also. So he'd contacted them. The three of them had discussed her at length. She was a virgin, but a willing fuck. She would respect pack law, even though she seemed shy about fucking them all. He told the other two he would break her in, and bring her along sexually until she was ready.

She was *his*. But pack law was pack law. By taking charge, he'd established himself as alpha male and her one true-mate. Lukas and John hadn't argued. Damn good thing too. It wouldn't do for a respectable pack member to kill his own kind.

At the moment, killing was the furthest thing from his mind. Her hot, torturous breath wreaked havoc on his neck. More than anything he wanted to fuck her *right now*, not carry her away to some isolated spot. His cock burned with a fever he'd never experienced before.

Fucking her silly would be okay. The act would consummate their mating, make her his. But he wanted her to crave fucking him, beg for his attention. She would love his cock; he could tell by her actions. Her breathing was quick and excited, her breasts smashing against his chest with each inhalation. Lust had swarmed in her eyes since she'd learned they would be mates. If he handled this right, she would beg him to fuck her again and again.

So he had to be slow, no matter how desperately he wanted to pound her cunt until his cock couldn't take it anymore.

He found a quiet area between the trees with a thick patch of needles carpeting the rough ground. When he put her down, his cock strained painfully against the pressure from her lithe body. She wouldn't know of his personal torment, of the sweet pain she inflicted. Taking Sophie had been his dream for years. He would do it right.

He ripped his sweatshirt off and spread it over the needles, making a bed for her.

"I want you to lie down for me." He worked to sound calm when he wanted to force her to her hands and knees. To grip her ass, then pound her holes while she screamed with pleasure.

Sophie knelt, looking up at him with wide eyes. "What are you going to do?"

She sounded shy, her cockiness from before washed from her and replaced with a demure gaze that turned him on more than if she stroked his cock for him.

It would be easier to show her than tell her. She'd spread her legs, showing off her glorious cunt; its roundness shone with come. Her sweet scent filled the air around them. She smiled and her cheeks turned a beautiful shade of pink. He wanted to kiss her, to tell her what she did to him. To tell her that he had wanted to fuck her for years. But he knew if he got any closer to her right now, he would pound his cock into her and gain only his satisfaction. Tonight would be for both of them.

Tonight he would make her his for life.

"Touch me, Nik," she whispered.

He hadn't meant to hold her in suspense while enjoying the feast before him. The beauty of that smooth cunt, widespread slender thighs, round breasts with hardened nipples made her appear a sacrifice, offered to him, and he wished only to worship her beauty for a moment.

If he touched her, he would ravish her, he was sure of it. Maybe conversation could keep him sane, help him remember how innocent the vixen lying willing in front of him really was.

"Why do you shave?" He ran a finger over her slit.

Her body lurched when she reached for him but then hesitated, and her fingers drifted through her silky blonde hair.

His cock twitched, aching for attention. Instead, he parted her pussy lips, touching her round little clit. Her hips bucked, and she locked her legs around his arm.

"Nik. Oh my God. Nik."

Her orgasm swelled through her, filling him with pride and powerful desire. She would come for him with the simple stroke of his finger. And the way she cried out his name… His adorable bitch would be a wonderful playmate.

"You are so beautiful." He couldn't help but praise her.

When he reached for her knees, she fought him, peering at him from beneath lowered lids like a wild animal, but finally spread her legs far apart.

"Good girl. Now answer me." His fingers trembled while he stroked her pussy, fighting to be gentle, aching to dive deep into her heat, to feel her muscles clamp around him.

Keep talking. Maintain control. "Tell me why do you shave?"

"I like how it looks," she said on a gasp, her mouth forming an "o".

He had no argument there. He spread her pussy lips, and her outer muscles clamped on to his finger, soaked him with her hot cream. Her body prepared for another orgasm; her thighs quaked, her breath came in gasps. He slid his finger inside her, imagining his cock sliding into her sweet hole. She was so fucking hot! Her lusty fire burned through him.

"Do you watch yourself, baby?" He worked another finger into her cunt. Her come seeped out and covered his hand.

He fucked her with his fingers, pumping them in and out of her wet pussy. Her breath came quick and shallow, and she grabbed her breasts, pulling and squeezing them so that her caramel-colored nipples poked up at him.

"Sometimes."

His balls tightened. Pre-come leaked from his cock. He couldn't endure the sweet torture any longer. He struggled one-handed with his fly, until he freed his cock from the unbearable confinement. The cold air did nothing to calm the savage heat pulsing through him.

In and out. His fingers drove deep inside her tight cunt, then slid out slowly, her muscles fighting him. He wanted to bury himself in her heat. Need made it hard to keep his thoughts straight.

Spreading her legs further, she rocked her ass back and forth, prompting her orgasm. "Oh. Nik." She rode his fingers, thrusting wildly and clamping down. Hot come drenched his hand. It took more strength than he'd thought he possessed not to come with her.

Her pussy crushed his fingers, then another spasm forced them from her pussy. He couldn't pull his gaze from her tiny hole, which remained open for him briefly, before it clamped shut again and thick cream spread toward her ass.

"I have to taste you, baby." He adjusted himself between her legs, waiting until she seemed to register what he'd said and looked down at him. "Before I fuck you, I want to lick your come out of you."

He willed her to hold his gaze, to watch him feast upon her while he lapped at the come dripping down toward the virgin asshole that would be his alone. When he finally lowered his mouth to her hot cunt, her rich cream intoxicated him. The folds of her pussy were so smooth, so tight.

"Nik. Oh. Shit." She shook her head from side to side, her pretty blonde hair splashing over her face.

He grasped her legs, spreading her, while feasting on her pussy. Shoving his tongue deep, he tasted her fresh lust, and her muscles contracted around him. Then, lifting her higher, he teased her tight ass with his tongue, nipping at it and watching her come pool at its entrance.

He rimmed her sweet asshole, imagining how tight she would be when he fucked her there.

His cock reared like a dangerous creature, swelling and surging with angry life. He needed inside her, needed her tight heat around him. Needed to possess every bit of her.

"I can't wait any longer," he murmured, half to himself. "I'm going to go mad if I don't fuck you soon."

"You're going to make me your bitch?" Her whispered words wrapped around him, reminding him of the age-old pack tradition. Her virginity, her pureness, her first experience. All of this they would share, making her his bitch, marking their unity.

When he lifted his head, she studied him, her gaze heavy with lust and curiosity. Her blonde hair was tousled around her face, tangled from her fingers running through it. Her blue eyes looked wild, filled with desire and hesitation that made him crazy with lust. Then uncertainty pooled in her eyes, and her mouth puckered into an almost pout. Her body stiffened; her worry fragranced the air around them.

"My sweet little *lunewulf* bitch. My glorious Sophie." Needing to kiss that growing pout off her face, he smiled and raised himself over her. "You've been my bitch for years."

She gasped, a radiant shade of pink warming her cheeks — he'd said what she wanted to hear. Sophie wanted to be his bitch.

He wouldn't let her down. Their union would be forever. He would bring her his kill, lay it at her feet, adoring her always.

And he would make sure she knew she belonged to him first and foremost.

His cock burned with a fever to prove himself to her. Knowing she wanted him, needed him, he placed his swollen cockhead against her pussy. She opened her mouth to cry out, and he captured her plea with his kiss. Her tongue darted out but retreated just as quickly.

Her shyness excited him. The eagerness of her body filled the air around them with her luscious scent. Hot and ready. Her mouth was sweet, a mixture of cheese, potato chips, and the lingering tang of beer. He fucked her mouth with his tongue, lost in the desire to pound into her pussy.

"Fuck me, Nik." She breathed her words into his mouth. "I've waited forever for this."

So had he.

He pressed his engorged cock against her virgin cunt, feeling her open to him. Drenched and ready to be his bitch, she would mate with him, and following the tradition of centuries, be one with him for life.

She was so tight…so wet…so fucking hot he knew he would lose his mind. "Dear God. Sophie."

Control. He had to maintain control or he would change while inside her. Sophie wasn't ready for that.

He slid deep, breaking past her fragile hymen. Her heat devoured him, turning his body to flame, drawing out the predator from within his soul.

"Mine, Sophie." Molten fire scalded his throbbing cock. She felt so fucking good. "You are mine!"

She tensed briefly, reminding him to keep his movements slow. "It's okay, baby. Tell me if I hurt you," he whispered, and ran his tongue across her shoulder. The scent of outdoors clung to her salty skin.

"Don't stop, Nik. I need this so bad. Fuck me. Please fuck me." Her cries echoed through his feverish mind, added to the chaos of his enraptured senses.

He arched his back, his bones straining to change, aching to grow and divide. Focusing on her, he lowered his head to suck a puckered nipple, testing it with his teeth.

She wrapped her legs around him, holding him to her. Her come soaked his balls and dripped over his thighs. He fed off the warm scent of her sex, gliding long and slow, deep into her.

"Nik. Help me. Nik!" She stiffened, yet another orgasm rippling through her, squeezing his cock with her pussy.

So tight. And although he wanted her ass, wanted her mouth, her pussy…*his* pussy…clenched, *milked* him. He quit fighting back the explosion and his come burst forth, his soul melting into hers.

Chapter Four

Nik held himself above her while his cock slowly contracted. His scent enveloped her, powerful and dominating, yet caressing her at the same time. He'd tried to be gentle, but he'd nearly ripped her in two. Terrifying heat burned through her body, scouring a path to her pussy. Her pulse pounded in her cunt.

Emotions ran through her too fast to understand. Her heart hammered in her chest, matching the pulse in her pussy. Her bones stretched, muscles rippling and contorting around them, veins lengthening and thickening as blood surged through her to the beat of the beast within.

I'm no longer a virgin.

Nik had taken her, mated with her. She couldn't turn back, couldn't alter her future. Tradition dictated when two werewolves mated, it was for life. She belonged to him, and he belonged to her.

So many thoughts bombarded her at once. She would have to tell Grandmother. Nik would come for her, take her to his den. Everything would be different now.

But those thoughts paled next to the onslaught of her newly fucked body. Her pussy burned, felt stretched and swollen, satisfied yet aching. Her nerve endings tingled with excitement and fear.

"I am your mate," she whispered, but her words came out garbled. She'd begun the change, and her mouth had stretched.

She looked up at Nik. So gorgeous, so in control. Those dark blue eyes watching her, protecting her. He smiled and slid his cock out of her. The cold of the night left her as warm fur covered her skin. She rolled over, hurrying to her feet, wanting to dance under the moon. To celebrate with her new mate. But fucking left her weaker than she'd realized; her legs wouldn't support her.

Either Nik sympathized with her inability to prevent the change, or deemed it a good idea to be in fur, because he'd allowed the transformation from man to werewolf to sweep through his body as well. He moved over her, nipping and holding the back of her neck until she could stand.

When her strength returned, he nudged her and grabbed their clothes with his mouth. At the command of her mate, she trotted through the woods. She pranced alongside Nik, working to keep up with his longer stride.

Her pussy throbbed and come matted the moon-colored fur along her inner thighs. She was all too aware of Nik next to her, his strong alpha scent permeating the air that tickled her nostrils. His powerful muscles rippled under his thick white coat, creating waves of motion that reminded her how hard he had made her come.

Desire lanced through her. She wanted his cock inside her again already.

Her pussy ached, but there were other things they could do. She could suck his cock, lick her come from his shaft and taste their mingled juices.

Or he could take her ass—an act so raw, so carnal, she almost came again just thinking about submitting to him in that way.

* * * * *

The party had broken up when they reached the backyard of Johann's place. Nik changed first, his legs growing, white fur becoming flesh. Taut, smooth skin glistening with sweat.

Her muscles altered and fur disappeared. The night air clung to her skin. Her beautiful *lunewulf* body, powerful and pure like the glow of the moon, transformed into her human form, slender and petite…and cold.

"Nik?" She reached for her clothes, then pulled her sweater over her head.

He stood there naked, clothes in hand, watching her. The darkness added a predatory hardness to his features, accentuated his well-defined chest. He looked dangerous, a wolf to reckon with.

She breathed deeply, gathering her thoughts. "I'm going to have to do…" His brooding gaze rested heavy on her. "Well, you know. I'm going to have to fuck Jonathan and Lukas too."

He looked away and tugged his jeans on without commenting.

"I'm loyal to the pack." She chewed on her lower lip, searching for words to tell him she was scared, but willing. Nik supported pack law, and she would support him. "I don't want you to think I'll be trouble for you as a mate."

Nik glanced around the yard. It was quiet now though the scent of beer still drifted through the air. They were alone. The cars were all gone, and she didn't smell any werewolves around them. She met his gaze when he looked at her.

"I don't want to share you with *anyone*." He gripped her arms, his tone harsh, biting. "Do you understand me? You are mine!"

Oh, hell yes! Her heart pounded in her chest at his ferocity. She hadn't realized until now his true feelings.

"I'm all yours. And don't you ever forget it." She had to know what he planned to do about her two other mates. "But what about pack law?"

"We'll honor pack law." She studied his face. So handsome and sexy, so sure of himself.

She wanted to walk into that powerful chest, and let his hands caress her worries away. But he had something to tell her; she sensed it.

"I've made arrangements."

Her stomach tightened into knots.

He rubbed her arms, soothing her, obviously smelling her nervousness, and then cupped her face with his hands. "And we'll do this only if you agree."

"Do what?" The plans he'd mentioned to Lukas! Oh... Her mouth went dry.

"I've arranged for Jonathan and Lukas to meet us at my place tomorrow tonight. They'll fuck you, but I'll be there. You are my mate, and I will know what my mate experiences."

It suddenly seemed hard to breathe. All three of them would be there with her? Her heart pounded in her chest. Would one fuck her, and then another? Or maybe she would do all of them at once? Nervous energy raced through her, but she couldn't deny the spark of arousal spawned deep in her gut by the thought of a foursome. Three men fucking her at the same time…

Could she handle it? Did she want to handle it?

"You'll be there with them?" She wanted Nik with her, *if* she decided they would all fuck her together.

"No wolf will touch you without my being there." His words shuddered through her, so determined, so full of passion, so caring.

"I need to think about this." She didn't want to let him down, but what if she couldn't go through with it? She needed time to sort her thoughts.

"This is how it has to be, Sophie." He pulled her to him, his heartbeat pounding against her breasts. "We can have you mated to all of us, and then I will say when they may breed you."

When his arms wrapped tight around her, she relaxed into his heat. Her pussy was sore, yet the aching desire to fuck him surged through her once again.

Nik would never break pack law, no matter how much he must want to keep her to himself. She knew how he felt. If it weren't for him, she wouldn't mind fucking the other two wolves — they weren't unattractive or cruel. But she loved Nik. And only Nik. She would do this, for the breed, for her pack, but mostly she would do it for Nik. It would be easier for him this way, and easier for her too to have him there.

"Yes. This is how it has to be," she whispered.

Chapter Five

Sophie's pack mates lined two rows of folding chairs, intentionally placed so Grandmother could pace in front of the pack. Nik leaned against the wall, his arms crossed over his broad chest, his expression serious. He respected Grandmother as pack leader and had always backed her decisions. But at the moment, Sophie didn't give a damn about pack policy, or any decisions the pack needed to make.

Some dispute had broken out between two dens, and Grandmother mediated while each den voiced their complaints.

"She is enjoying this too much," Elsa, sitting next to her, whispered. Her revulsion filled the air with its rank odor.

Sophie shushed her, not wanting her sister in trouble with Grandmother again. Elsa seemed to have a knack for getting the old bitch riled.

She turned her attention back to Nik. His presence seemed to have a power over her; just looking at him made her wet with desire.

Jonathan Abram, who would also be her mate, stood on one side of him. Since he was a couple years older than Nik, she'd never really spoken to him. She took the opportunity to study the werewolf, letting her gaze wander over his lanky physique. He wasn't an unattractive man, just quiet. He didn't go to the parties or bars she went to. His longish blond hair curled up under his collar at the back of his neck. Right now he wore his leather jacket, but she'd seen him working in town with construction crews and knew he had several tattoos.

What kind of lover would he make? Her senses swirled within her, a fluttering of butterflies settling in her stomach.

You will find out when you go to Nik's place tonight.

"Are there any other matters we need to discuss?" Grandmother's shrewd gaze passed over the werewolves, who scuffled in their seats, anticipating the end of the meeting. The old bitch nodded at the silence. "Then this meeting is adjourned until next month."

Grandmother Rousseau took her time sitting in the large upright chair, but Sophie sighed with relief. She almost floated out of her chair when Nik began working his way toward her.

Will you enjoy watching me fuck the other wolves?

"Sophie." Gertrude gestured to get her attention.

"Grandmother wants to talk to you. She told me to send you to the study." Gertrude drew a line across her throat with her finger. Sophie was in trouble for something.

The butterflies in Sophie's stomach formed a thick knot. What the hell had she done now?

She glanced over toward Nik, who had stopped to talk to a couple of den mates. With a sigh of defeat, she headed to the study to face the battleaxe by herself.

* * * * *

"I am told you are now Niklas Alexander's mate." Katherine Rousseau didn't waste time.

Sophie offered her hand to help her grandmother into a chair. Grandmother Rousseau eased back, releasing Sophie's hand only to slap her on the ass.

Sophie squealed before she could stop herself. "What?"

Her grandmother's spanking didn't hurt as much as it humiliated her. "Nik is one of my chosen mates. What have I done wrong?"

"Sophia." Grandmother clasped her hands in her lap, pursing her lips. Her hard stare made Sophie more nervous than she cared to admit. "You mated with him in the woods, like a common tramp. You are a Rousseau!"

Sophie stood facing her, silent. It wouldn't be dignified to ask where her grandmother got her information. The best thing to do was get the reprimand over with.

"Would you have him breed you in the woods?" Grandmother curled her lips in disgust, and then apparently realizing Sophie had no response, she sighed and shook her head. "Niklas Alexander approached me this morning. Of course he lives with his brother, but he informs me that he has applied for a loan and should have you two in a home of your own within the month."

Nik is buying me a home? She wanted to jump for joy. Her dream man would take her away from her grandmother's restrictions…and she would have her own home.

"I guess until then, the two of you will live with me. At least that way I can assure that things are done properly."

Sophie cringed at the thought of Grandmother standing at the foot of the bed, supervising the way they fucked. "I'll let Nik know you've offered your home." She hoped she sounded gracious.

Grandmother nodded. She was excused. Good thing. She needed to get out of there, out of the house, and as far away from Grandmother as she could.

Where was Nik?

As was tradition, covered dishes brought from each den were set out on tables that had been set up in Sophie's absence.

Elsa stood next to the long table of food with an empty plate in her hand. "I'm supposed to tell you Nik ran into town with a few men, and will pick you up when he comes back."

"What did Grandmother want?" Gertrude walked up behind them, eying the food.

"Nik and I mated last night." Sophie stared at the food, her stomach too knotted to enjoy any of it. "And of course, Grandmother seems to know all the details."

"She probably jacked off to all the details." Elsa picked up a chicken wing, then dropped it back on the platter.

"You are so disgusting." Gertrude rolled her eyes, helping herself to a wing. "That old bat probably dried up years ago. But anyway, congrats Sophie. One down and two to go."

And I will do both of them tonight. Fear gripped her, but a nervous excitement seemed to tingle through her bloodstream as well.

She would mate with her two other wolves with Nik by her side. This was the best way.

"I think being forced to take three mates is disgusting." Elsa put her plate down on the edge of the table. "No one is going to *tell* me who to mate with."

She tossed her long blonde hair over her shoulder and marched away. Sophie shook her head. "She is going to get into shitloads of trouble with that attitude."

Glancing around the large room, Sophie didn't see anyone she wanted to talk to. She had no idea how long Nik would be gone. Maybe a run was in order. Her bones stretched and popped at the thought, and her teeth pressed against the inside of her mouth by the time she reached the back deck. She stepped around a group of cubs, who played around their mothers; some were in their fur, some only half-changed.

"Would Nik approve of his mate running alone?" Johann stopped her halfway across the deck.

Elsa stood next to him, and from the look on her face, it seemed she'd just been intercepted by their cousin as well.

"He isn't here for me to ask." Sophie straightened. She wouldn't let her older, way-too-protective, distant cousin ruin her day any further. "And it's not like I'm a single bitch anymore."

Elsa curled her lip. Clearly her little sister had just been reminded of the etiquette for young female werewolves. *Good little werewolves only run with an escort*, Grandmother had told them more times than Sophie cared to remember.

"I'll join the two of you on a run." Johann pulled a cell phone off the clip on his belt. "And I'll let Nik know that his mate is in good hands."

Sophie sighed and nodded. At least she could get away from her demented grandmother. That would be something at least.

Chapter Six

The instinct to dominate, to claim again what was his, ran rampant through Nik's senses. Instead, he took Sophie's hand and led her up to his brother's house. Her cold skin confirmed the nervousness he smelled on her.

He closed the front door behind them.

"Are we alone?" She looked up at him wide-eyed.

"For right now we are."

"I don't think Grandmother will be too pleased if I'm out all night." Her lower lip came out in a perfect little pout. He could just imagine sliding his cock through those puckered lips. "How — how long until Jonathan and Lukas arrive?"

"You are my mate. I can keep you out for the rest of my life if I wish." He loved watching her crystal blue eyes grow wide and something akin to gratitude wash across her face. "Jonathan and Lukas are down the street at the bar. They'll come over when I call them."

"Oh." She chewed on her lip. Would she back out? "I guess they don't want to wait down there all night."

"We can take all the time you need." He brushed his finger over her cheek to her lips. He couldn't deny the small desire that she would back out, refuse to be with any werewolf but him. But he also ached to see her fucked by the other wolves, coming until she couldn't see straight.

She opened her mouth, and her tongue darted out to taste his fingertip. Those pouty lips moved, sucking in his finger. Then her tongue swirled around it, springing his cock to life.

His sweet little bitch didn't realize the peril she put herself in.

"I have something for you." Reluctantly he slid his finger from her hot mouth, and headed for the dining room.

"What is it?"

He held out the bag, and watched her pull out the sexy lingerie he'd decided she would wear tonight.

"Undress for me, Sophie." He sat on the couch, ignoring his cock which strained furiously, suffocating from the pressure of his jeans. "I want to see you in lingerie I bought for you."

"I love lingerie." Her delighted smile told him he had done the right thing.

She would wear what he'd bought for her, bought for his adorable bitch.

She moved to stand in front of him, placing the bag between them on the coffee table. Gripping her sweater, she pulled it up, exposing skin. Plump perky breasts spilled over her pink lacy bra, and blood boiled in his brain.

A slow smile played on her lips. She was enjoying herself. Her delicate fingers traced invisible lines over those mouth-watering mounds of flesh and lace. He wanted her to give him a private show, finger-fuck herself…beg him to take her first, before the other werewolves showed up.

She unzipped her jeans, torturously slow, then slid them down her long, slender legs.

His heart pounded in his chest, the beat matching the throbbing in his cock. "Damn, Sophie." The pointed edge of his incisor pricked the inside of his mouth, and the taste of blood urged his beast to come forth. "I can't be responsible for my actions if you're going to tease me like that."

She looked very pleased with herself. "But you told me to undress for you." The coy tone in her voice sounded almost wicked.

"So I did." He wanted to help her, but knew if he moved, he would never see that outfit on her.

She slipped out of her panties and lace bra, then pulled the black silk corset over her head. It fit snug around her waist; her perfect tits brimmed over the cups. She eased the matching thong up, covering her smooth cunt. Her scent drifted toward him, creating raw hunger as she situated the material evenly between her legs.

"I can't wait to fuck you. And I am going to enjoy watching you be fucked." The time had almost arrived. He needed to prepare her.

But she was so fucking hot he had to take a moment simply to stare at his perfect little bitch.

Her blonde hair streamed over her shoulders, and crystal blue eyes searched his face, needing his approval. Her creamy skin had not one scar from scrapes in the woods. Her narrow waist and petite muscles gave her the perfect shape.

"Turn around." She obeyed instantly, giving him a wonderful view of her round ass.

He stood slowly—the lethal weapon in his pants made movement difficult.

"So fucking perfect." He cupped her ass, spreading it to reveal the black elastic that ran over her asshole and disappeared into the damp pussy that he craved to eat.

"I want your two other mates to see you in all your perfection." He dragged her back to him, pressing her ass into the swollen heat of his cock.

He breathed in her lusty scent, kissing her silky hair. The swell of her breasts offered a view that would torment a saint.

"You'll enjoy watching?" She leaned back, her breath warm and moist against his skin.

God. How he would love to fuck that cleavage.

He reached for his phone, clipped at his waist, and Sophie stiffened in his arms. She turned quickly, panic permeating her scent. Sensing her instinct to run kick in with a vengeance, he grabbed her.

"It's okay, my sexy bitch. We'll get through this together. I have a feeling you're going to love being fucked by all three of us at once."

Chapter Seven

Sophie couldn't breathe. Her heart beat with a frantic craving to run, to let the change surge through her so she could protect herself. She wanted to bury her face in Nik's powerful chest and confess to him that she wasn't ready.

"Go into the bedroom, my sweet little bitch." He turned her around and gave her ass a gentle swat.

Her legs trembled while she walked to the bedroom. She'd only been in this house a couple times, and prayed she wouldn't stray into the wrong room. She needed the privacy of his room, a sanctuary. Even if the wolves would join her soon, just a few minutes alone might soothe her ragged senses. Her mouth seemed dryer than sandpaper, and her palms were too sweaty. How could she mate with three men when she was on the verge of panic?

She brushed her fingers over the first door she came to. It opened easily under her touch. The darkness didn't hinder her, but her arms and legs seemed weak and shaky. Calming her breath proved impossible, but she managed to climb on to his bed and sit in the middle of it, absorbing the stillness of the room.

Baritone voices crept toward her. *They were here.* Her other two mates had arrived.

Someone turned on the light, stealing the comfort of shadows. She spun around on her haunches, her heart pounding in her throat, even while her pussy swelled and throbbed. She gasped for breath. Nik stood alone in the room, slowly removing his clothes.

"I want the light on, my precious mate." His tone soothed, calmed her.

She took slow deep breaths, urging herself to relax.

"I want to see them fuck you, and I want to watch you come for them."

All of them fucking her, their cocks all buried deep inside her... Her pussy quivered in crazy, nervous anticipation. "I don't know if I can do this," she whispered, even though she couldn't deny the arousal spreading through her with feverish delight.

Her nipples pressed hard against the fabric of the corset. The smell of her lust filled the room.

Nik stripped and stood before her, his cock swollen and eager to stake its claim. Her mouth filled with moisture, and the room seemed to get warmer as she knelt on his bed, watching him approach with that hard cock sticking out in front of him. She glanced past him for a moment, but didn't see either of the other men.

"We're doing this together, Sophie." Nik seemed to sense her unease. "I want to make sure you are calm first, and ready for them."

"What should I do?" Could she do this?

Her body seemed a frenzy of emotions. She'd had so much fun fucking Nik, and Lukas and Jonathan were to be her mates according to pack law. Over the years she would fuck all of them many times. She reminded herself of the reasons why this was a good way to break the ice. All of them accepting her, and she learning the pleasures each of them offered. And Nik was right; they were doing this together. He was her alpha male, her protector, and the wolf she loved.

"Relax." Nik smiled down at her, crawling on to the bed and pulling her to him. His mouth covered hers, his kiss hot, branding her...possessing her. He ran his tongue over her lips, leaving her mouth warm and moist. "We'll all enjoy you and offer you pleasure like you've never known before. All you have to do is enjoy it."

All I have to do is enjoy it. She repeated his words like a mantra, slowing her breath, concentrating on his touch. Nik lowered his head, and ran his tongue in between her breasts. She arched into him, grasping his shoulders. He gripped her ass, kneading and spreading it, exposing her cunt.

Fire raced through her wherever he touched her. The need for him to fuck her consumed her senses.

"I want you to suck my cock," he whispered into her chest, and she nodded her head, although she knew he couldn't see her do it.

Anything. She would do anything. He pressed her back on to the bed, the heat in his lust-filled gaze singeing her skin. He moved closer so that his cock, with its bulging dark purple veins, hovered over her face.

Powerful hands clasped her head, tangling through her hair. The musky scent of his sex intoxicated her. Her mouth seemed suddenly too wet, as if she drooled in anticipation. She stretched her lips around his head, then touched his tip with her tongue.

His cock filled her mouth, the soft skin moving against her lips. She gagged on his size, the thickness of him pushing, pressing, until he reached the back of her throat.

"Damn, Sophie. Your mouth is hotter than I dreamed it would be."

So he'd dreamed about this too? His encouraging words assured her he didn't mind her gagging just a bit.

Sophie closed her eyes to savor the salty taste of his pre-come. He stroked his cock back and forth over her lips, while her tongue swirled around his hardness, exploring him while he fucked her mouth.

His cock, and his rhythm. That was all she knew.

Then hands gripped her thighs, easing her thong off and spreading her legs. Fingers touched her overheated pussy lips. She gasped and bucked when a smooth tongue soothed the sweltering ache and sank deep inside her pussy.

Still more hands squeezed her breasts, pulling and kneading them. The clasp of her bra unsnapped. Fingers pinched her nipples, sending waves of electricity through her, making her pussy tingle and throb.

Someone lifted her hand and wrapped her fingers around a cock. Immediately she traced her fingers along its thick shaft. The velvety skin slid under her fingers, and hardness turned to steel as she stroked and rubbed. Running her fingers over its head, she learned the thick roundness of it. When a drop of come moistened her finger, she spread it over the shaft, liking the hot slipperiness of it.

"You are so fucking hot." Lukas' voice—so this must be his cock in her hand. She explored further, stroking and pulling, discovering what she could about her thick, brawny mate.

Pleasure swept through her when he groaned in appreciation.

"She is absolutely beautiful." Jonathan, her tattooed construction worker, spoke from between her legs. Then he lowered his mouth and sucked on her clit, sending sparks flying behind her eyelids.

Sophie couldn't believe how wonderful all this attention and praise made her feel. Worries and unnecessary panic crept away, and she flexed her inner thighs, pressing her pussy into Jonathan's mouth. Fiery moisture trickled down the crack of her ass as he sucked.

Her tongue danced around Nik's cock as he drove in and out of her mouth. Her jaw stretched, and her lips tingled, the source of his power freeing her, making her strong...a temptress capable of pleasing three lovers.

She moved her fingers up and down Lukas' cock, more and more confident of her actions as his steel shaft bucked in her hand.

These three men would be her mates for life. Their groans assured her she would be able to give them pleasure, and her building orgasm that she would receive it from each of them.

"My little bitch is enjoying herself." Nik's voice sounded husky. His personal claim made it clear she would answer to him first in this tetrad relationship. It also made her feel loved.

He pulled his cock from her mouth. She licked her numb lips, her mouth swollen but full of the flavor of her mate's cock.

Nik moved her away from the other two men, propping her up so that she sat on the bed. She blinked, looking at her three wolves then. All of them were naked, their eyes glazed over with lust. The scent of sex hung thick, an aphrodisiac.

"I want you to straddle Lukas, baby," Nik told her.

Lukas crawled on to the bed next to her. Reaching for her, he kissed and squeezed her extra-sensitive breasts as she climbed over him.

"That's it, baby," Nik encouraged her, his hand stroking her hair. "Slide that drenched pussy of yours over his cock. I can smell how wet you are."

Sophie reached between her legs and positioned Lukas' cock at the entrance of her cunt. Her muscles opened to allow his cock to impale her. Pressure grew inside her womb, quickening, building as he moved deeper and deeper inside her.

"Nik." She needed to know he was near. "Oh. Shit."

"That's it, Sophie." Nik moved behind her.

Nik's hands gripped her hips, pushing her down further on to Lukas' cock. She screamed. White light exploded in her head...her cunt ruptured into blazing liquid heat.

Feeling a weight next to her, she glanced through her sexual fog. Jonathan had moved over to the side of the bed.

"Take Jonathan's cock," Nik whispered into her hair. "I want you to suck it just the way you sucked mine."

She turned toward Jonathan, momentarily fixated by the dark blond curls covering several tattoos on his chest. She lowered her gaze to his long cock, which seemed to stand proud, showing its eagerness to know her.

She dropped to all fours, allowing Nik to control her fucking Lukas' cock. Jonathan slid his swollen head and shaft over her tongue, filling her mouth as she closed her lips around him. His cock tasted so damn good.

Nik's hands teased her sensitive ass, lubricating her small, tight hole with her own cream. She pushed against his finger, creating a rhythm of her own. She fucked Lukas' cock and Nik's finger, incredible pressure building in her ass, another orgasm begging to explode.

Her asshole stretched, fire spreading through her.

"You like this, don't you baby?" Nik's growls made her wild with the urge to fuck and be fucked. An aching need grew deep inside her to experience all of them inside her at once.

Six hands caressed and stroked her feverish body, her mates surrounding her, invading her senses with their individual scents. She sucked and fucked, her brain reeling with the sensual overload. Nik fucked her ass with more than one finger now, stretching her further, pressing into her as she rode Lukas' cock.

And then they were moving her again. She barely heard the instructions this time, but simply adjusted her body to allow Jonathan underneath her. His cock slid into her, hitting a point deep inside her that Lukas hadn't touched. She howled at the intensity of it, and Nik's strong hands stabilized her, keeping her from falling over. A rush of heat flooded through her, setting off a craving for more.

"Suck on Lukas' cock, little bitch." Nik's encouraging whisper seemed to fill her head, become her own thought. When she opened her mouth to the thick shaft that had just been in her pussy, the taste of her own come greeted her, thick and creamy, bittersweet and exciting.

Nik's cock pressed against her ass, spreading electrical tingles of pleasure. Her cunt stretched around Jonathan's long shaft, while her tongue darted over Lukas' thicker cock.

Searing pain surged through her, taking her strength. It seemed the bed had fallen out from underneath them.

The pain faded and Nik's cock slid deep into her ass, her own come soaking the entrance and easing his way. The two cocks, Jonathan's in her pussy, and Nik's in her ass, stretched her, rubbed her, building an ache beyond bearing. She throbbed from the pleasure/pain, ready to come, but not wanting it to end.

She sucked furiously on Lukas' cock, and he gripped her head, either slowing her or simply controlling the direction. She didn't know, and was beyond caring.

"I'm going to come," Lukas cried out, holding her mouth to his cock. Hot seed spilled against her tongue.

The salty taste filtered through her like a drug. She lapped at it until he pulled his cock free, leaving her mouth empty, bereft. She panted and held herself on her hands and knees, needing to come — unable to do anything but accept the multiple sensations ripping through her as Nik and Jonathan pounded her cunt and her ass.

Jonathan pulled out of her pussy, then shoved his cock into her mouth. She didn't question his actions, but sucked and tasted the cock that had just fucked her cunt, drank and swallowed the hot explosion of his come.

"It's my turn, baby." Nik gripped her hips roughly, thrusting hard, then his hot seed spilled into her ass.

She felt almost light enough to float when he slid free and his hot come leaked from her burning ass.

Jonathan took her into his arms and hugged her. "You're wonderful Sophie. I'm lucky to have you as a mate."

"You are absolutely beautiful." Lukas offered her a shy smile.

She grinned, her vision blurry and her lips too swollen and tingly to form words. Strong hands pulled her back, and she found herself cuddled into Nik's warm embrace.

"You did it, my sweet bitch." Nik's breath tickled her ear. "You're the best mate I could ever dream of having."

She lay there, sated and limp. All she could do was smile when she heard Jonathan and Lukas say their goodbyes.

The bedroom door opened and closed, but she didn't move. Nik's warmth spread through her as she lay next to him, his strong arms wrapped around her. She was almost asleep when he whispered against her cheek.

"I love you, my sweet Sophie."

She opened her eyes and stared into the face of the man she had adored for years. "Oh Nik, I love you too."

About the author:

All my life, I've wondered at how people fall into the routines of life. The paths we travel seemed to be well-trodden by society. We go to school, fall in love, find a line of work (and hope and pray it is one we like), have children and do our best to mold them into good people who will travel the same path. This is the path so commonly referred to as the "real world". The characters in my books are destined to stray down a different path other than the one society suggests. Each story leads the reader into a world altered slightly from the one they know. For me, this is what good fiction is about, an opportunity to escape from the daily grind and wander down someone else's path. Lorie O'Clare lives in Kansas with her three sons.

Lorie welcomes mail from readers. You can write to her c/o Ellora's Cave Publishing at 1337 Commerce Drive, Suite 13, Stow OH 44224.

Also by Lorie O'Clare:

Lunewulf: In Her Blood
Lunewulf: In Her Dreams

DEVLIN DYNASTY: RUNNING MATE

Jaci Burton

Chapter One

"Jason Devlin is over there."

Kelsey Harper spun, looking where her father was pointing. Her heart picked up its usual frantic pace whenever Senator Devlin was mentioned.

Leave it to Walter Harper to spot a news story in the making. As owner of *The Washington Oracle*, D.C.'s popular newspaper, her father had a nose for a scoop better than anyone she'd ever seen.

She'd grown up around newspaper publishing and reporting, and wouldn't dream of ever doing anything else. Kelsey lived for digging up a story, especially one related to politics, although she preferred to get the goods on corrupt politicians and what they did behind the scenes.

"I don't see him," she said. Who could find anyone in the packed ballroom? She'd just arrived, so she missed dinner and the Senator's speech and wasn't certain he was still around. When Jason Devlin made an appearance, a sellout was guaranteed. Chances were, he was wherever the biggest crowd was gathered.

The man was simply news, and not only because of his principles. He was the "it" man in politics, and was talked about as a potential Presidential candidate. He was also one of the best looking men she'd ever seen. Six-foot-two and lean, with thick, dark hair and eyes the color of fine whiskey. A gorgeous man with a body to die for and a brain to match. His features screamed 'aristocrat', from his tanned, angular jaw to his straight nose. The most important thing about him was his single status. A perfect package, available for the one woman who could manage to snag him.

Not that Kelsey was interested in snagging him. She just wanted to uncover his secrets.

In Washington, D.C., and especially politics, everybody had a skeleton or two in their closets.

Skeletons sold newspapers. Lots of them.

"He's looking longingly at the elevators," her father said. "My guess is he's hoping for a little privacy."

"Perfect." She'd been waiting forever to corner him for an interview. With his rabid, overly protective staff, no way was she getting any one-on-one time with him. At least, not the regular way. "I'm going to get up to his floor before he does, then block his doorway until I get an interview."

"That's my girl." Her father winked and kissed her cheek.

Kelsey grinned and slipped away toward the private elevators leading to the penthouse. She stopped as she saw a security guard escorting an attractive woman off the elevator, a sultry, big-breasted blonde in a tight, short dress that hid none of her assets. From the way she was arguing with the guard about what a huge mistake he was making, she wasn't one bit happy about being removed, either. Must be another Devlin groupie.

Kelsey waited until security was out of sight, then eased into the elevator and pressed the button for the penthouse. She glanced at her reflection in the mirrored walls of the elevator. The long, strapless black gown hugged her curves like a mummy's wrapping. Not really her favorite choice of clothing. Shorts and a halter top would have been more to her liking.

She applied some lipstick and tucked her chin-length hair behind her ears, comparing her appearance to the Playboy centerfold who'd just been escorted from the elevator.

Not even close. She had decent-sized breasts, but they certainly weren't as impressive as the blonde's. Her waist dipped in nicely, but she had a little more prominent hippage than Miss "I Eat Carrots For Breakfast, Lunch And Dinner".

At least she had nice green eyes with a little rim of blue around them. Her father had always told her that her eyes were her best feature. She wasn't certain if that was a true compliment or his way of playing down the rest of her, which was, sad to say, only average. From her brown hair to her not-model-sized body, she really was as nondescript as they came.

Then again, when had she ever cared about how she looked? Just because she'd attended these functions for two years and not once had Jason Devlin noticed her. Which didn't mean she should be concerned about her appearance.

After all, she was only planning to interview him, not fuck him.

When she reached the penthouse, she peeked out the elevator door, breathing a sigh of relief that no security guards manned the hallway. She slipped out and positioned herself near the window by the door to Devlin's suite, determined to confront him and refuse to take no for an answer. Tonight, she'd have some one-on-one time with the elusive senator.

The sounds of sirens outside blared in the distance, an everyday occurrence in the nation's capitol. To Kelsey, they were like a comforting lullaby. She'd cut her teeth in a gritty newspaper office and had learned everything about the business from the ground up. After her mother died when she was a toddler, her only influence had been her father, and he knew nothing about raising girls. He'd taught her about journalism instead.

Of course, she'd never tell her father, the award-winning Walter Harper, that her favorite things to read were the gossip rags. He frowned on her exposés about the nation's elite, but always let her print whatever she thought best. Because of his faith in her, she never pushed the envelope between what was news and what was trash. Every story she wrote could be backed up with proof.

Tonight, she hoped to garner a little "truth" about Jason Devlin. If he was feeling generous, maybe he'd invite her into his suite for an interview.

* * * * *

The ballroom was filled to capacity at The Sadler, D.C.'s premier hotel. Senator Jason Devlin had shaken so many hands and smiled for so many cameras, his hand and face hurt.

All he really wanted to do was run through the park until the tension knotting his muscles relaxed. That wouldn't happen for awhile, though. Instead, he was dressed up in his usual monkey suit, smiling, talking and fending off reporters' questions about why the capitol's most eligible bachelor wasn't dating anyone.

They probably thought he was gay. Good. Better than knowing the truth about him. It wasn't like he could date just anyone. Not with his quirks and strange life. Someday, maybe, he'd find a mate. But he'd choose from those among his kind, never a human. Humans couldn't be trusted to keep his secrets.

He searched the crowd for his cousin, Brandon King, who was also his aide and beta. He needed to get out of here and couldn't break through the throng of people following him around as if the very act of taking a sip of champagne was newsworthy. Sometimes he hated this part of his job. Politics was for change, not headlines, but because of his looks and the fact he was thirty-eight years old and single, his love life made more news than his policies.

Brandon approached and sidled beside him. "Need out?"

"Hell yeah. I need some goddamn space."

Brandon nodded and signaled for security to move the crowd aside. Leaning in toward him, Brandon whispered, "I've got someone up at the penthouse waiting to meet you. One of ours. Thought you looked a little high strung tonight and could use a little relief."

"Thanks." Great. Nothing like having his beta pimp for him. But Brandon knew everyone in this town, including their own kind. Despite the fact he was alpha of the pack, he didn't socialize with them that often. There were just too many of them and he was too damned busy.

But his beta was right. He needed a good fuck. It had been too long and the urge was hitting him on a regular basis. Too bad he couldn't just do it the normal way and meet a woman first, get to know her, and then get physical.

There were definitely drawbacks to being a werewolf in a prominent position in politics.

After several handshakes and goodnights, Brandon turned to the crowd and said, "The Senator has some phone calls to make. How about giving him a break and letting him through?"

Leave it to Brandon to give them a smile and a wink and flash the old baby blues. The single women in the room naturally gravitated to Brandon and his California surfer boy good looks, surrounding him like a bunch of ready-to-mate she-wolves. Grateful, Jason slipped through the crowds with the two guards leading the way, breathing a sigh of relief when the elevator doors closed behind them.

When the doors opened, security stepped out, doing their usual search and destroy mission. Jason rolled his eyes, wondering what they'd think if they knew he could kill them both in seconds with his bare hands. He hardly needed their protection.

They motioned him out of the elevators and down the hall to his suite. Sitting in one of the chairs near the windows was a beautiful vision. She stood and smiled as he approached and his heart stopped for one brief second.

Beautiful women were in abundance at these events. But this one was striking. Chin-length sable hair, wide emerald-green eyes, and a curvy body that had his cock twitching to life like a divining rod searching for water in the desert. She looked familiar, too. Maybe he'd seen her with the pack before, but just hadn't noticed. Although how he could miss someone so stunning was incomprehensible. He'd have to remember to thank Brandon.

Later.

"You're not supposed to be here," one of the guards said in a low warning voice.

"It's okay," Jason interrupted. "I was expecting her. She's with me."

Her eyes widened in surprise, but she didn't say anything.

"Come on in." He slipped the key in the lock and pushed the door open, then dismissed the guards, shutting the door behind them.

His eyes immediately adjusted to the lack of light, focusing on the woman's silhouette. Her fragrance permeated his senses—not perfume, but she must use some kind of strawberry-flavored body wash. That sweet smell coupled with her natural, musky scent took his cock from semi-rigid to "get me the fuck out of these pants now!" in an instant.

"Um, Senator, are you going to turn the lights on?" she asked, her voice low and gravelly. His balls tightened.

"In a minute. Call me Jason."

There was something different about this woman. Her scent, the way she stood rigid in front of him. The she-wolves of the pack were always primed and ready for fucking, especially by the alpha. Normally he wouldn't get the door shut before one would be unzipping his pants and wrapping her lips around his shaft. So far, this one hadn't moved. Maybe she was new to the pack and uncertain about his expectations.

"If you're afraid, don't be. I don't have any rules. However this goes is up to you and me."

"I don't think you—"

"Shhhh," he whispered, stroking her bare shoulders and trailing his fingers down her arms. She shuddered, and the wolf in him wanted to howl at her response. He scented the beginnings of her arousal. Though she wasn't aggressive as the she-wolves he was used to fucking, her innocence and hesitance enticed him more than if she'd done a striptease and given him a blowjob in the hallway. Although he really liked the visual that thought conjured up.

"No, really, Senator, what I'm trying to say is—"

He turned her around and slid his fingers into her silken hair. "I don't want to talk any more. I want to kiss you, lick you, taste you all over. Then I want to spend the rest of the night with my cock so deep inside you that we don't know where I end and you begin. And I want that now."

To prove his point, he covered her mouth with his, silencing the words that she was about to say.

Chapter Two

Somewhere in the recesses of her mind, Kelsey knew she should object. She should push Jason Devlin away and slap him soundly. Then, she should hightail it out of there armed with a hot story about how she was nearly assaulted by the senator.

But as his tongue stroked hers intimately, evoking responses she'd never felt before, she knew that wasn't what was happening here at all.

Clearly, he had been expecting someone else. He probably thought Kelsey was that blonde bimbette who'd been escorted out the door. She could have spoken up at any time, yet she hadn't, so she had no one to blame but herself.

Maybe the blonde was a prostitute! Holy hell, did he have to pay for sex?

No, no that couldn't be it. Jason Devlin could have any woman he wanted with a snap of his fingers.

So, who was the blonde?

Oh hell, how could she even think when he was kissing her like this?

Kelsey inhaled Jason's heady fragrance, an earthy scent that made her mouth water. Her mind was awhirl with sensation as he stroked his lips over hers and gently assaulted her mouth. He held her tight against him, evidence of his arousal rocking against her sex. Her panties moistened with juices she couldn't control.

Dammit, she didn't want to be turned on by this stranger. She was a journalist. Impartial, uninvolved. She was only here to get a story.

If she didn't stop him, she'd be getting a story all right, but not one she could put into print.

"Your arousal fills the air around me," he whispered against her ear. His tongue darted out and traced the outline of her ear, his teeth closing over the lobe just enough to make her shiver. "Tell me your name."

Her name? What the hell was her name, anyway? "Kel...Kelsey," she managed, the word dragging out of her mouth on a ragged breath as he cupped her breast.

She'd only known Jason Devlin as a poised, cool politician. What she'd seen in press releases and interviews and on television, anyway. The man holding her in his arms was not the cool and calm senator. This was a man whose body was taut with tension, muscles straining under his tux. A man whose touch was hot, burning her from the inside out.

"I'm going to strip that dress off you, Kelsey," he said, and she knew he wasn't asking for permission. He reached behind her, found the zipper and slowly tugged it down. His knuckles brushed her spine, sending tingling shots of pleasure to her sex. If ever there was a time for her to put a stop to this, now was it.

But she couldn't. Her body had stormed to life in a wicked way, demanding satisfaction from an aching need she hadn't even known she possessed. She'd been lost from the moment she'd laid eyes on Jason walking toward her. Their eyes had met and he'd focused on her as if a hunger possessed him, and she was the meal to satisfy him. In that brief second, his eyes had turned from light whiskey to darkened, golden amber, his movements like the slow, sensual grace of an animal predator.

In that instant, she'd tumbled headlong into a vortex of spiraling sensations that knocked the common sense right out of her.

"Your skin is so soft, like dipping my fingers in cream," he murmured, palming her buttocks and squeezing gently. When he tugged on her thong, she was afraid she'd pass out.. When he slipped his fingers in the cleft of her ass, her knees buckled.

"Ahh, so you like to be touched there." To prove he was right, he rubbed the puckered hole with his index finger. "I wonder what else you like, Kelsey."

She panted into his chest, wanting to rip his clothes off with her teeth and beg him to fuck her. "Jason, please," she pleaded, shock registering her whimpering voice in the foggy recesses of her mind.

"Yes, Kelsey. I'll give you everything you want. But first, I want to get you comfortable."

She shook her head, unable to fathom that they still stood just inside the front door. Before she could move her feet, he swept her into his arms and strode quickly through the darkness.

Did he have night vision? The drapes were closed and she couldn't see a damn thing, yet he walked with a brisk purpose as if he could see clearly.

He laid her on his bed. She sat up, trying to clear the sensual haze that made this seem more a dream than reality, but then he opened the drapes, his body bathed by the moonlight.

With a quick tug, he discarded the bow tie and shrugged out of his tux jacket. Keeping his gaze firmly fixed on her, he unbuttoned his shirt and pulled it off, giving her a tantalizing glimpse of a very fit body. A light dusting of dark hair covered his chest and trailed downward, disappearing over his taut abdomen and reforming again right above the waistband of his pants.

She sucked in a breath, unable to believe this whole night was happening. Later, when logic smacked her in the face like a D.C. winter day, she'd regret this. Now, she wanted it more than anything.

Her gaze fixated on that slowly traveling zipper. He spread the material apart and slipped his pants off.

No underwear. God, was that sexy. His rigid, thick cock jutted forward from the nest of black curls surrounding it. She looked up and met his half-smile, her heart slamming against her ribs.

"Stand up," he commanded.

She slipped off the bed and stood before him, holding her gown up with her hands.

"No," he said, pulling her hands away. "I want to see."

The dress fell to her hips. If she'd been the skinny blonde bimbo, it would have fallen gracefully to the floor. Figured.

Jason stepped forward and reached for the dress, sliding his hands over her hips. The dress pooled at her feet. He spanned her waist and pulled her against him, her nipples registering the contact with his chest by pebbling into tight, aching peaks. Threading his fingers through her hair, he gave a light tug that sent a flash of need directly to her sex. Her cunt throbbed, demanding satisfaction.

"You're beautiful," he murmured, pressing his lips against hers. His tongue slid inside her mouth and swept alongside hers, making her weak with his tantalizing strokes. He drew back and grinned, then took her hand and led her to the window.

They were in the penthouse, the top floor, and his room didn't overlook any other hotel, so she knew she wouldn't be seen. Yet standing there naked in the moonlight made her feel vulnerable, even though Jason stood in front of her.

He cupped her breasts, sliding his thumbs lightly over her nipples. She bit her lip to keep from crying out. When he bent over and took one peak into his mouth and licked it like a lollipop, she thought she might faint. What started out as a slow, seductive laving of her nipple turned harder. He tugged the bud between his teeth, then captured it firmly between his lips, flicking his thumb over the other nipple. She was dying from the myriad sensations threatening to send her into the throes of orgasm before he ever got near her pussy.

Jason released the bud, watching it with rapt interest as it puckered and stood firmly erect. Then he took the other in his mouth and did the same until she threw her head back and moaned.

When he dropped to his knees, her eyes flew open and she looked down, watching him lean forward and nuzzle against the light dusting of fur on her mound.

She inhaled, the heady scent of sex permeating the room.

"I'm wondering if you taste as sweet as you smell." He leaned forward and touched the tip of his tongue to her clit, then lower. She tensed, nearly climaxing on the spot at the feel of his hot tongue stroking along the soft folds of her pussy.

"Mmm, baby, you taste good." His voice was as tight and hot as she felt deep inside.

Kelsey couldn't take much more of this torture. She'd been on the verge of orgasm since the moment she'd watched Jason's approach from the elevator, sensual intent written all over his face.

And now that face was buried between her legs doing delicious things to her body. She tangled her fingers in his hair, wanting his attention but unable to form the words. He looked up at her, his eyes dark, smoky, mysterious. A smile tugged the corners of his lips upward. "Not yet, Kelsey. You have to let go for me. I want to taste it."

She couldn't bear it, needed him to fill her, to fuck her into oblivion. Anything but this slow torture that drove her to the brink. But seeing his dark head buried between her legs, listening to the sounds he made as he lapped up her liquid desire, and experiencing the mind blowing pleasure of his hot tongue, was more than enough to send her over the edge.

Her legs shook with the force of her orgasm. She cried out, burying her fingers in his hair as wave after wave of delicious sensation pummeled her. Her world spun on its axis and she fought for breath, finally able to do no more than pant and tremble.

Jason stood and pulled her into his arms, driving his lips down over hers. She licked her juices from his mouth and held onto him as he lifted her and moved to the bed, lying down next to her on the satin-covered mattress. His cock, still heavy and thick, brushed her thigh, reminding her that there was more to come.

Good lord. If fucking him was as good or better than what she'd just experienced, she might not survive it.

Chapter Three

Jason drew in a long breath, mesmerized by the woman lying next to him.

Kelsey was no lupine. He'd known immediately by her scent and the fact she hadn't at least partially transformed. She had a beguiling innocence that he hadn't seen in a very long time, and that part of her drew him in a way he couldn't understand. Didn't want to understand. But he felt bonded with this stranger, and he'd never felt that connection with another woman.

Ridiculous, since she couldn't be his pack mate. Kelsey was a human.

He didn't know who she was, and damn if fucking her went against every rule of the pack, but she was here, he wanted her, and he was going to have her. He'd deal with the consequences later.

Brushing her hair away from her face, he stared into her luminous eyes. Such awe and curiosity in their depths, he wondered what she was thinking. Probably better not to know.

Her lips were full, yet natural, not like so many of those thin-lipped socialites who paid a plastic surgeon for a mouth like Kelsey's. His balls drew tight at the thought of those prominent lips wrapped around his throbbing cock. He'd bet she was damned talented with a blowjob and made a mental note to find out.

Later.

Right now, he needed her hands on him, needed to be inside her, more than anything else.

"Touch me, Kelsey."

She reached for him without hesitation, a smile curving her lips as she wrapped her warm hand around his cock. He growled and fought back the urge to change. The feral need to possess, to mark this woman, was almost more than he could bear. His blood stirred and blasted through his veins, centering on all the nerve endings in his cock and demanding his full attention.

"Yes. Stroke it like that." Her hand moved over his shaft and he gritted his teeth to keep from coming right then. No fucking way was that going to happen.

When she reached underneath and massaged his balls, he sucked in a breath and grabbed her hand. "Unless you want me coming all over that sweet body of yours, you need to stop."

She grinned. "I wouldn't mind watching you come."

His balls drew up tight at the thought of her gaze focused on his spurting cock. "You may yet get your wish, but not right now."

"Are you sure?" She slipped her fingers underneath the twin sacs and rubbed the sensitized patch of skin between his balls and ass.

"Shit!" God, he loved the feel of her hands on him, but he had to stop her from touching him like that. He grabbed her hand and wound her arm around his neck, then lifted her leg over his hip, positioning his cock against her sweet pussy. Her juices were like molten lava pouring over the head of his shaft, singeing him, compelling him to plunge into her heat.

He wanted to make this last, prolong that first moment, but damn if he could wait. He parted her folds and with one thrust, buried his cock inside her.

Unable to hold back his growl, he snarled and buried his face in her neck, tasting her, scraping his teeth against her skin as her cunt fit itself around his shaft and squeezed. He moved against her, loving the way her pussy grabbed him as he partially withdrew, then drove in deeper.

"Oh, God!" she cried, tangling her fingers in his hair and tugging hard.

Yes, just the way he liked to fuck. A little hard, a little rough, with his woman giving as much as she got. But he purposely held back, not wanting to frighten her. She was, after all, human, and didn't understand the pack ways of sex. The last thing he needed was word getting out that Senator Jason Devlin liked it a little rough.

It was hard not to pound his cock inside her, to turn her over and place her on all fours so he could enter her from behind and lock onto her neck and shoulder with his teeth. He felt his claws unsheathe and by sheer force of will tucked the beast within him away.

Instead, he concentrated on the sensations of her pussy surrounding his cock, the hot little whimpers she made when he moved a certain way. Her nails dug into his shoulders when he quickened the tempo.

It was music to his ears when she said, "Harder, Jason."

He reached for her buttocks, pulling her tight against him and grinding his pelvis against her clit. She shrieked and sank her teeth into his upper chest in response. Oh, yeah, he liked that.

Wetting his fingers with the nectar pouring from her cunt, he searched the cleft between her buttocks and, sensing her need, slipped one moistened finger inside her puckered hole.

She grunted like an animal, her ass tightening around his finger as he probed deeper. He felt the spasms surround his cock and he plunged with more force. She screamed, flooding his shaft with her climax.

The sensation was so intense it was difficult to hold back. She rocked against him, raking her nails down his arms and crying out his name. Giving her no time to rest, he continued to stroke, listening to her breathing turn to gasps of pleasure as he wound her up again.

When her body tensed, soft whimpers escaping her throat, he knew she was ready to let go again. He sank his finger all the way into her ass and flooded her pussy with his come, taking her over the cliff with him.

For a while, the only sounds were their raspy breaths. Jason stroked Kelsey's hair, kissed her forehead, her pert little nose and her generous mouth, then wrapped his arms around her, more content than he could ever remember being.

Something felt right about holding her in his arms, about the way she fit so perfectly against his body. The moment he'd come in her, she became his.

And that brought about a dilemma of epic proportions. He'd never intended to mate with a human. In his line of work, a human who discovered he was a werewolf could be disastrous. There was no way he could trust someone outside the pack.

He didn't even know anything about her. But it was time he found out, because if his feelings were true, he'd just bedded his pack mate.

* * * * *

Kelsey sighed, content to listen to the sound of Jason's rhythmic heartbeat against her ear. His body was so warm she didn't even need the sheet over her, despite the blast of cold air from the room's air conditioner.

She supposed her theory that the reason D.C.'s most eligible bachelor was unattached was because he was gay had just been thrown right out the window. If Jason was gay, he'd just given her an Oscar-worthy performance in bed.

Her nipples tingled at the thought of what they'd just done, of how he had awakened a wild response that was foreign to her. In his arms, she'd felt untamed. She'd wanted to bite him, scratch him. Hell, she'd wanted to howl at the moon!

Wouldn't he have thought her bizarre if she'd done that?

Then again, he hadn't exactly been gentle with her, either. And she'd had the feeling that he'd been holding back. Perhaps there was more to Jason Devlin than she surmised.

Maybe he was really kinky! Had some bizarre predilection for whips and chains, nipple clamps and floggers.

She grinned at the thought of offering herself up as a research sacrifice. Wouldn't that make interesting press? *Senator Devlin Takes a Walk on the Wild Side.* She couldn't suppress the giggle at the thought of that headline, even though the idea was ludicrous.

"What's so funny?"

"Nothing."

"So, having an orgasm makes you laugh?"

She looked up at him, her heart doing flip-flops as she gazed into eyes the color of dark amber. "You didn't hear me laughing when I was screaming my head off, did you?"

His eyes heated with renewed desire. "No, I didn't."

She resisted the urge to sigh like a lovesick schoolgirl, but truly the man was gorgeous. More than his appearance, he exuded a confident sexuality that most men couldn't possibly carry off. Jason did, though.

"Kelsey?"

"Yeah?"

"Tell me about yourself."

Uh oh. So much for great sex and that warm afterglow. As soon as he found out who she was, she'd be out the door on her ass faster than she could say "hot off the presses".. She pushed away, sat up and faced him, swallowing hard to get the words out. "I'm a reporter for *The Washington Oracle*."

The hand stroking her thigh stilled. "A reporter."

"Yes."

She much preferred the heated looks he'd given her earlier to the cold narrowing of his eyes now.

"I thought you were…"

She waited, but he didn't finish. "You thought I was what?"

"Never mind. I just assumed you were someone else when I saw you waiting for me."

The blonde, no doubt.

"Did you come here for a story?"

Might as well come out with the truth. "Actually, I snuck up here tonight and waited outside your suite, hoping you'd grant me an interview."

Jason slipped from the bed and combed his fingers through his hair. "I guess you got that interview, didn't you?"

She arched a brow and crossed her arms, irritated that he would think she'd trade sex for a story. "That's rather insulting. Do you see any tape recorders or cameras on me?"

His gaze traveled over her in an insulting manner, but it had the opposite effect on her unruly body. Her nipples hardened to sharp points, a fact that wasn't lost on him as his gaze focused on her breasts. "Not unless you've got some mini-recorder tucked away inside you."

She rolled her eyes and slid from the bed, pushing past him to search for her dress.

"Where are you going?" he asked.

She got to her knees and grabbed her dress from under the bed. "I'm leaving."

"Why?"

"Because you think I fucked you for a story." He refused to budge when she stood, holding her dress up in front of her. "Get out of my way!"

When she tried to move past him, he reached for her hand. "Wait, Kelsey."

"What?"

"Stay with me."

"Why?"

He shrugged. "I don't know. Honestly, I should throw you out of here. A journalist and a politician don't make good bedfellows."

Sure hadn't stopped him from taking her to his bed. Then again, he hadn't known she was a reporter. Would it have made any difference? "Then why ask me to stay?"

"Like I said. I don't know. I'd like you to spend the weekend with me. I have a need to get to know you better."

There went her throat again—dry as a desert as she tried to swallow. "The weekend?"

"Yeah. I have a private place in the Poconos. Will you go up there with me?"

This was the chance she'd waited two years for. The opportunity to get to know Jason Devlin.

"But our time together is off the record. You have to agree to that. I don't need a sexposé printed in the next *Oracle*."

Like she'd actually discuss her intimate sex life in the newspaper. Not likely. But could she really spend that much time with him and not report on anything she saw, heard or experienced? How was she supposed to find out what skeletons lurked in his closet if she wasn't allowed to open the closet door?

She'd figure out a way without compromising her integrity. This was too good an opportunity to pass up. She'd had her fun with him. Now the work would begin.

"Sure, I'll go with you," she said, trying to convince herself that the only reason she agreed was to find out

more about Jason Devlin, not because she felt anything for
him.

Chapter Four

"Are you insane? Do you know what could happen if a human, let alone a reporter, found out about you? About all of us?"

Jason listened to Brandon rant through the cell phone, conscious of the fact that Kelsey sat only a foot away from him in the limo. "I'm aware of the ramifications."

"And yet you're still going to Pennsylvania with Kelsey Harper."

"Yes, as a matter of fact I am."

With a sigh, Brandon said, "You're the alpha. I guess you know what you're doing. But I'm going on record as stating that I think this is a really bad idea."

"Duly noted." He ended the call, hoping Brandon wasn't right.

He glanced over and watched the way Kelsey worried her bottom lip with her teeth. He wanted to do that for her, then lick her lips and move on from there. He shifted as his cock twitched, wondering how he could be turned on by the sight of a woman in jeans and a silk shirt.

A shirt that hugged her breasts and caressed her hips, the same way the jeans fit her. Snug, showcasing her thighs and long legs. He remembered the feel of her skin and wanted to strip her down and fuck her right there in the limo.

It had been twenty-four hours since he'd bedded her, and already he itched to be inside her again. His lust for her was full force now, and nothing could stop it until the alpha drive had been completed. Until she was truly, completely his.

Considering she didn't even know he was a werewolf, he figured dropping that bomb on her today wasn't a particularly smart idea.

What would she do when she found out? Run? Stay? Write an article about werewolves in the capitol?

Christ, too many "what ifs" running through his head, and none of them good. He needed this weekend to relax and get Kelsey used to the idea of being with him. Then, very cautiously, he'd let her in on his secret.

After all, she was going to help him build the Devlin dynasty. At least his part of it.

The Devlin werewolves had been in existence for centuries. And they weren't the only ones. Someday, if he had his way, laws would be passed to protect his kind so they were treated the same as humans. Right now, society wasn't nearly ready for them to come out.

He wished they had time to stop off at his parents' house in Boston, but knew now was not the right occasion. They would welcome Kelsey, as would his sister, Chantal. His brothers—Max, Conner and Noah—might be a bit more skeptical. Who knew how they'd react to his selection of a human as pack mate? The Devlins' goal was to branch out across the United States and unite with other packs. Then mate with other werewolves, not with humans. He'd just blown that directive right out of the water, hadn't he?

Jason had already done his part in Washington, and he knew Max was getting ready to head to New Orleans and do the same thing. It was going to take time, but they had all the time in the world. None of this was going to happen overnight. It would take time and finesse and more than a little fighting to take their places on top of the packs. Devlins were alphas. Always would be, no matter where they located. They'd set up nationwide, and run the packs the way they should be.

"I've never been to the Poconos," Kelsey mumbled, her gaze focused on their climb into the mountains. "It's breathtaking."

Yes, she certainly was. While he enjoyed the seclusion of his private place, he was more interested in catching sight of her breasts, or her creamy thighs, or the way she licked her lips. Adjusting his burgeoning erection, he said, "Yeah, it's really nice in the fall. I'll have to bring you up here after summer's officially over, when the leaves start to change."

She looked at him, eyes widening. "In the fall?"

"Yeah."

"That's like a month or so away."

"Yes, it is. Your point?"

"Um, I guess I don't really have one." She quickly turned away, but not before he caught the blush staining her cheeks. Kelsey really was an enigma. One he intended to research in depth this weekend.

The limo pulled up to the wrought-iron privacy gates, their driver clicking a button to electronically open them.

No press lurked at the gates. Good. So far, he was fairly certain no one knew what had happened with Kelsey. He wanted some time alone with her before the papers found out and started hounding them.

Reporters would make good wolves. They hunted in packs and surrounded their prey, refusing to let go until they finished the kill.

"Wow. This is impressive."

He followed her gaze to the one-story ranch house. Sitting high atop a green hill, it overlooked the lake on three sides. He loved this place. It was perfect for a private getaway, and he was surrounded by everything he loved. Water, lots of fish, and tall, thick, woodlands to sprint through.

The driver carried their bags into the house, then left them alone. Jason led Kelsey inside, his tension level dropping as soon as he inhaled the fresh mountain air.

"This is stunning, Jason. I love the wood floors and the simplicity of the décor. I'm not one for elaborate furniture or having a lot of 'stuff' clutter a room."

She noticed. He didn't like things ornate or busy, although a lot of women he knew would want to redecorate. "I'm glad you like it. Would you like a drink?"

"Love one."

He led her into the kitchen and opened a bottle of champagne. "Would you like to sit in the hot tub and watch the stars come out?"

Taking a sip, she said, "Okay. Let me unpack and get my suit on."

"You don't need a swimsuit to get in the hot tub with me. I've seen you naked already."

She opened her mouth to say something, then closed it and nodded. "Okay. Let me go put on a cover-up for when we get out."

He grinned and directed her to the master bedroom where he'd had the driver put their luggage. Might as well not give her ideas that she'd be sleeping anywhere this weekend other than with him.

He set the champagne in an ice bucket next to the hot tub, then brought out a bowl of strawberries. The staff did a great job getting everything ready at the spur of the moment, then discreetly disappearing. Of course, he paid them quite well to do so.

After stripping, he slipped into the tub, the steam rising off water that was set at a perfect temperature to counteract the chill in the air tonight.

The slight breeze brought the earthy, woodland scent to him. The urge to shift and run into the woods nearly overpowered him. To smell the fresh pine needles, dig into the soft earth and run as far as he wanted to. That was one of the reasons he loved it here. He had privacy to be himself.

Well, normally he would. But not right now. He forced away his primal needs, knowing he couldn't change right now. Not with Kelsey here. That would have to wait until he figured out a way to break the news to her. He wondered how she'd react, since he knew basically nothing about her. He'd had Brandon run a background check on her. Twenty-five. Daughter of the owner of *The Oracle*. Mother died when she was three. No brothers, sisters or other relatives. Journalism degree. Worked at the newspaper since she was a teen.

Nothing in her background clouded his desire for her. Except maybe the journalism part. He couldn't very well prevent her from doing her job, but he could hope that when she found out about him, she'd keep his secret.

His career depended on it.

He heard Kelsey's footsteps on the wood deck and turned. She wore a thick robe that covered her upper thighs, but gave him a glimpse of long, slender legs. The robe had parted, a tantalizing peek at her generous cleavage his reward.

"Water feels great. Come on in."

She walked toward him and sat on the edge, trailing her fingertips along the surface of the water. "It's cold outside."

"It's hot in here."

She seemed reluctant to move.

"I won't bite." Well, he would, but not 'til later.

"I'm having second thoughts about all this, Jason."

His heart dropped to his feet. "About getting in the hot tub, or about something else?"

"About all of this. You and me. This is all happening so quickly. Why am I here with you?"

"Because you said yes when I asked you to come up here." He felt her hesitation, knew that she was troubled about something.

"I know what I said. But why did you ask? You could bring any one of a thousand women up here. Beautiful women."

"I did ask a beautiful woman to come up here with me. And she said yes. Now get in the hot tub."

A sparkle glinted in her eyes and her cheeks tinged pink, as they seemed to always do when she was embarrassed. Did she not know how stunning she was? A full, curvy body and long legs, she was the epitome of perfect woman in his eyes.

Scooting her legs over the edge of the tub, she dipped them in, then untied the robe and let it fall to the floor of the deck before sliding quickly into the water. He'd caught only a glimpse of her body.

She sat across from him on the other bench. "Come over here, Kelsey."

"I'm fine right here."

She was shy! But why? After what they'd shared last night, she'd have no reason to be coy with him. But uncertainty filled her. He sensed every one of her conflicting emotions.

"You stay there, then." He stood and grabbed their glasses of champagne, handing one to her, then grabbed the bowl of strawberries and sat next to her. Before she could say a word, he grabbed a strawberry and popped it into her open mouth.

She bit down and chewed. He watched the way she licked her lips. After taking a sip of champagne and swallowing, she said, "That's good."

Indeed it was. Jason knew that any movement of her lips was going to forever give him a raging hard-on. "Does kind of explode in your mouth, doesn't it?"

She arched a brow. "Yes, as a matter of fact it does. Very sweet, too, and the champagne gives it an added tanginess. Here, you try." She slipped one into his mouth and he closed his lips over her fingers, tasting her along with the strawberry.

They spent a few minutes feeding each other. Soon, they'd polished off the bowl and the bottle, then laid their heads back and looked up at the sky.

The three-quarter moon pulled at him, making his blood turn hot, his skin tingle with anticipation and his cock hard as the trunk of the woodland trees. In a couple days, the moon would be full and he'd have to announce his mate to his pack. He didn't have nearly enough time.

"Tell me about your job," he asked, wanting nothing more than to sink his cock into Kelsey's tight heat right now, but afraid she'd think all he wanted from her was sex.

"It's all I've ever known, and everything that I love. My dad used to bring me to *The Oracle* offices when I was little. By the time I started school I was already making up stories in my head. When I learned to write, I kept a journal. My dad tells me I was always interviewing someone, and I was pretty darn good at it, even when I was six."

"Your father thinks very highly of you. That's admirable."

"Thanks. I think pretty highly of him, too. He's been my inspiration, always after me to seek the truth and not be afraid to tell the world about it. That as long as it was true and could be backed up with evidence, then it was our obligation to report it."

The truth. When he told her about himself, it would be true. When she watched him transform, it would be evidence. Would she tell the world about him, about his family?

Why couldn't he have chosen someone outside of politics or journalism as his mate? Why did it have to be so instinctual? It wasn't like he could change his mind about Kelsey. The moment he'd met her the magic had caught hold of him and held, and he knew she was the one. He could no more turn his back on his need for her than he could cut off his own limb.

But he might very well be destroying himself by revealing who and what he was.

"What if you had a friend or relative with a secret, and that secret, while newsworthy, could also devastate their very lives? Because it was true and you had evidence to that fact, would you write about it?"

She sat up and looked at him, curiosity filling her green eyes. "Are you telling me you have a secret?"

Chapter Five

Kelsey wasn't sure she wanted to know the answer, but Jason's thinly veiled "what if" told her he was hiding something. Although she loved her work, sometimes she wished she wasn't a journalist, that she wasn't so consumed with getting a story that it overrode everything else in her life. This was one of those times.

"Me? No. I don't have any secrets to tell."

He was lying. She knew it, felt it, sensed that he wanted to tell her, but didn't trust her.

"Then why did you ask?"

He shrugged. "Curious, I guess. Must be difficult to know where to draw the line between what's newsworthy and what's just plain gossip."

His statement rankled her. "I don't gossip. Everything I print is based on solid evidence."

"Which doesn't necessarily mean it's the public's right to know."

She'd had that argument with critics of the press for years. "I guess it depends on what the public thinks they should know."

"I just think there are too many important things that could be printed. Unfortunately, the press oftentimes think that someone's personal life is more interesting than the good work they do."

Which led her to believe there was something in his personal life he didn't want anyone to know about. And he didn't trust her enough to reveal any of his secrets to her.

Not that she blamed him, but then again, her word was on the line. Her personal interest in him warred with the side of her that smelled a scoop. But a promise was a promise. "I gave you my word that whatever happens this weekend is off the record. If you have something to say, then say it and I won't put it in print."

He smiled and tucked a stray hair behind her ear. "If I have something to tell you, I will. But right now I want to enjoy the night with you."

The reporter in her wanted to press him for details, to finagle a way to get him to spill whatever secrets he held. The woman in her wanted to kick that reporter's ass right off the property so she could enjoy being with Jason.

Just once she wished she could turn the internal demons off. Couldn't she do that for one weekend? Simply enjoy being a woman in the company of a man who clearly desired her?

Jason moved to the other bench across the spa, pulling her along so that she faced away from him. He sat her between his legs and wrapped his arms around her middle.

"I like sitting here and looking at the lake. You can see the moon reflected in the water," he said.

She nodded, trying to focus on the clear lake in front of her, but her body was more tuned in to the brush of his arms along the underside of her breasts. "It's lovely."

Nuzzling her neck, he licked her gently. "Yes, you are."

Her nipples hardened and puckered as she shivered under his hot tongue. When he lightly nibbled her shoulder, she shuddered her next breath. His cock rose and pressed against her buttocks, hard, urgent as he rocked gently against her. She swallowed and licked her lips, feeling every movement he made as if it were the first time a man had touched her.

"Your body entices me, Kelsey. Soft skin, perfectly formed breasts and hips that make me want to dig my fingers into that sweet flesh while I pump my cock hard and furious inside you."

His words made her dizzy, his sensual teasing making her pussy quake with need for him. She moved her hands over his thighs, the crisp hairs there tickling her palms.

But there was so much more of him she wanted to touch, to taste. It might be her only chance to get this close to a man who so obviously hit all the right buttons for her, and she didn't want to regret a lost opportunity. Shifting to face him, she pressed her lips against his, tasting the sweetness of strawberries on his tongue. She entwined her tongue around his and suckled it, rewarded with his groan.

In turn, he gave her a passion-filled kiss that curled her toes, moving his hands over her breasts to gently pluck at her nipples. She whimpered as the sensation shot straight to her cunt.

She slipped off his lap and knelt on the floor of the hot tub, resting her hands on his outstretched legs. His thick cock was outlined in the water below, and she wanted to taste him. "Stand up, Jason."

He looked at her, his eyes dark as the woodland forests, but did as she asked, rising out of the water to stand in front of her.

Perfect. His cock stood inches from her mouth. She tilted her head back to make sure he was watching her. He smiled down at her, his eyes half closed, and watched as she enveloped his shaft between her lips.

"Christ, Kelsey, that's good." His hips jutted forward as he fed her his thick cock inch by inch. She wound her tongue around the head and licked the salty fluid from the tip, then drew him in deeper.

Cradling his balls in her hands, she massaged them lightly, pumping her mouth over his shaft and drawing him nearly out of her mouth, only to greedily suck him inside again. She laved every ridge of his shaft, enjoying the taste of him as much as she'd enjoyed the strawberries he'd fed her earlier.

A sense of power overcame her. She controlled him right now, with every swipe of her tongue, every suckle of her mouth, she was in charge of his pleasure. He rewarded her with his sharp intake of breath and the whispered words that told her he enjoyed what she was doing to him.

"Enough," he finally said, his voice husky and ragged. "I have to fuck you."

She smiled up at him. "Later."

He shook his head and dragged her to a standing position. "No. Now!" Without waiting for her response, her turned her around, pushed her toward the opposite bench. She reached for the edge of the hot tub, Jason positioning the front of his thighs against the back of hers. He nestled his cock near her sex, pushed her forward so her ass was up in the air, and slipped his hand between her legs, parting her folds and sinking two fingers inside her.

She cried out at the sweet invasion as he probed her cunt. Her juices poured from her.

"I want to make love to you slow and easy, Kelsey. I want to look into your eyes and stroke my cock inside you for hours on end. And I will. But not now. I've waited too long and I want to fuck you. Hard. Really damn hard. If that's not what you want, then tell me now."

She shuddered at the ferocity of his desire, relief washing over her that he wanted her as desperately as she wanted him. She craned her neck around to meet his hungry gaze and said, "Fuck me, Jason. Take it, just the way you want it."

With a low growl, he turned her around, dug his fingers into her hips and drove hard inside her. She screamed at the invasion of his thick cock and pushed back to meet his thrusts. Her pussy quivered and squeezed him as if determined to receive his life force.

Jason leaned over her, licking the middle of her spine and up, inch by inch, not once stopping the punishing momentum of his cock. She felt the rumbling growls in his chest as he pressed against her back, knowing then that he had changed from a cool, poised senator to an animal driven by primal lust and need.

She welcomed him this way, overjoyed that he trusted her enough to show her this side of him. And she revealed herself to him, demanding him to plunge harder, to hurt her. He offered up a deep, husky laugh and sank his teeth into her shoulder, his fingers piercing the tender flesh of her hips.

The pain drove her higher. A fierce howl tore from her lips as a blistering orgasm knifed through her. She couldn't move except to shudder and cry out, as Jason had pinned her in place with his teeth, refusing to give her ground. Tears welled and spilled from her eyes as the painful pleasure continued. She'd no more relaxed from the quaking climax than another came upon her. And still, he drove relentlessly within her, refusing to stop.

Her legs trembled with the effort to remain upright as the second wave arced within her. This time, he released her shoulder and howled into the night, pouring his seed deep inside her. His body shook as he rode out his orgasm, then collapsed against her. He continued to caress her, running his hands over her thighs and between her legs, tenderly stroking her pussy until desire sparked again.

Jason lifted her into his arms and stepped from the hot tub, carrying her upstairs to his bedroom. She was still trying to catch her breath when he yanked the covers back and laid her on the bed, then crawled in beside her and pulled her against him.

Exhaustion claimed her, and for what seemed like only a few minutes, she slumbered. She awoke to the feel of Jason's fingers probing between her legs. She thought she had no more to give him, but she was wrong. Her sex dampened with each of his gentle strokes against her clit. He lazily caressed her, leaning on his elbow and watching her as she twisted and turned under his questing fingers.

"Look at me when you come, Kelsey. I want to see your face."

No, she couldn't. It was too intimate. And yet his gaze held hers as if by some unknown force and she let him have what he wanted. Her eyes widened as he slipped his fingers inside her and thrummed her clit with his thumb. She reached for his hand and drove his fingers deeper as she climaxed, watching the dark smile on his face as she cried out her fulfillment

He continued to gently stroke her, long past the time she had finally relaxed. She looked down at his hard cock, shocked to find her body responding once again.

"I can't," she whispered, afraid she was giving up her soul to him.

"You can, and you will. When I ask you for it, you'll give it to me. Every single time. Not because I demand it, but because you want to. The choice is yours, Kelsey. It's your will, not mine. You want this. You want me. You're mine."

She wanted to object, to scream at him that she belonged to no one but herself. But damn him, he was right. As Jason brought her to life yet again with his coaxing strokes along her aching slit, she knew that she'd fallen hopelessly in love with him.

Although she hardly knew him, no matter what skeletons he hid in his closet, she wanted him. As he took her again and again throughout the night, she gave herself willingly.

No man would ever elicit the same kind of response from her. Never had before, and never would again. She couldn't change her mind, couldn't walk away from him, and she'd never be the same person she was before she'd walked into his hotel suite that night.

It was already too late for her.

Chapter Six

After spending the weekend with Kelsey, Jason didn't want to let her go. By the time they'd reached Baltimore, he'd convinced her to spend the night with him at his place, determined not to let her out of his sight until he told her the truth.

She slept peacefully beside him after a wild night of lovemaking. He smiled and stroked her silken hair, amazed that he'd found a woman whose passions matched his own. Now he just had to figure out how to keep her.

He slipped out of bed and moved to the door leading to the porch. Compelled by the full moon, he knew he'd have to leave and meet the pack. They'd expect their leader to hunt with them. Already his body felt the impending change, the pull of the moon a force too strong to resist. Slipping on jeans and a T-shirt, he tiptoed out the back door, grateful that the park adjoined his property, one of the main reasons he'd bought this place.

Privacy assured them safety tonight. No one wandered outside in the middle of the night, especially in a deserted park, unless they were looking for trouble. Those hunting trouble tonight would find it.

Besides, wolfen magic allowed them to meet, make all the ruckus they wanted within the confines of the area, and no one could wander in after they started.

Exhilaration fired his blood. Not only did he look forward to the change, but he'd also met the woman he wanted to spend his life with. Their weekend together had been more than he'd hoped for. Kelsey wasn't just beautiful and sexy, she was smart, and not afraid to voice her opinions. He loved her sassiness. Arguing with her had been the second greatest thing about their weekend.

The greatest thing had been that, no matter what they'd been arguing about, as soon as he pulled her into his arms and fit his mouth over hers, the argument was over. She would crawl into his arms and kiss him back, pouring out the kind of desire that he'd never thought to find with a woman. Their lovemaking was powerful, intense, both rough and achingly tender. He'd never realized that being with one's mate could be this fulfilling.

He loved her. The only thing left to do was to work through the details of telling her what he was, and hope that she was as open minded about his secret as she'd been about every other subject they'd discussed this weekend.

She had to accept him, because he couldn't imagine life without her now.

No way was he going to let her go.

* * * * *

Kelsey woke with a start, turning over to reach for Jason. He wasn't there, but his pillow was still warm. She slipped out of bed, wondering if he'd wandered into the kitchen for something to eat. As she passed by the sliding glass door, she stopped, blinking to focus her still-sleepy eyes.

Someone was in the backyard. Her heart slammed against her chest as she recognized that sexy walk. It was

Jason, and he was heading towards the park that backed up to his property.

She glanced at the clock. Two a.m. What the hell was he doing?

He surely couldn't be restless. She was damned exhausted from their lovemaking, which had been long, passion-filled and eminently satisfying, as always. She'd slept better this weekend than she had in years.

Even if he couldn't sleep, no one in their right mind would enter the park alone in the middle of the night. But sure as hell, he disappeared into the trees.

Shit. She knew she shouldn't follow him, but dammit, this was just too weird. Curiosity won over caution and she hurriedly threw on her jeans and shirt, sliding her feet into her tennis shoes as she bounded out the door.

The park was a short distance from the back door, but she sprinted anyway, not wanting to lose him in the winding trails and dense woodland. She sucked in a breath of courage as she plunged headlong into the darkened woods. Though the full moon offered enough light, once she'd entered the park the tall trees and dense foliage prevented her from seeing much.

She couldn't hear any sounds to indicate in which direction he might have gone, so she tried to stay on the trail, hoping she'd run into him or at least figure out what he was up to.

A niggling feeling of foreboding came over her. She shouldn't be here. Something bad was going to happen.

Jason, dammit, why are you in here? What could you be doing? Whatever it was, it wasn't something he wanted anyone to know about. Nobody came to the park in the middle of the night. Nobody.

She should turn around and run back to the house and forget she ever saw him heading to the park. She loved him. Shouldn't she trust the man she loved?

A rustling to her left caught her attention. She froze, unable to move an inch for fear that someone would pounce on her. But after a full minute, no one came crashing out of the hedges. Then she heard it again.

Hell. Now what? It wasn't like she'd been smart and brought some kind of weapon with her. What was she going to do if someone jumped her? Kick him in the shin with her Nikes?

Really, Kelsey. You're going to have to learn to think first, react second. This was stupid.

Then she guessed she'd go on being stupid, because she headed left to follow the sound, her heart pounding against her ribs and sweat pouring from her.

She'd never been more scared, nor more curious, as she tiptoed through the hedges, staying low to the ground in case whatever she heard wasn't someone, or something, she wanted to notice her.

When she got to the other side of the thick bushes, she came upon a clearing. It was as if the treetops parted in the middle of the park to reveal the full silver moon overhead. A man stood in the center of the clearing with his back to her. She couldn't tell if it was Jason or not, but the body type was similar.

What was he doing here? He looked as if he was waiting for someone, but who?

Fine. She'd just stay out of sight and wait, too. Damn him, if he'd had something to tell her, he should have done so this past weekend when she'd sworn everything was off the record. Well, they were back in D.C. now, and all bets were off.

Pushing aside the guilt at the thought of writing anything at all about Jason's private life, she straightened and looked around, intent on finding a vantage point a little closer.

But when she started to step out of the bushes, a hand clamped over her mouth and she was drawn against a hard body behind her. Her scream was muffled as the hand held firm to her.

Just as suddenly, she was whirled around to face her attacker.

"Jason!" she cried, smacking him soundly on the chest. "You scared the shit out of me!" Her heart still raced and she felt dizzy and nauseous. She blew in and out slowly to calm the rush of adrenaline.

"What are you doing here?" he hissed.

"Following you. What are *you* doing here?"

"None of your business. Go back to the house."

How dare he tell her what to do? "I don't take orders from you. What are you hiding? Why are you here, Jason?"

"You don't want to know." He jammed his fingers through his hair, frustration evident on his frowning face. "Well, maybe you do want to know. Christ, Kelsey, I didn't want you to find out this way!"

"Find out…" She closed her mouth, looked at the man in the clearing, then back at Jason.

No. No way. It couldn't be true. Not after what she'd experienced with him this weekend. "Oh God. You're gay."

Jason's eyes widened. "Uh, no."

"Yes you are. You're meeting that guy over there for some quickie action or something. You just fucked me for appearances, so that I'd never report the truth about you. I could be your irrefutable evidence." The thought hurt. Way more than she'd wanted to. He'd used her.

"No, Kelsey. You're wrong. I'm not gay. For God's sake, were you there this weekend? You know what we shared."

She crossed her arms, fighting back the tears she refused to shed. "You're a good actor."

Rolling his eyes, he said, "Nobody's *that* good!"

That's what she'd thought, too. She was wrong. "Then tell me what you're doing meeting that man over there. If it's not for sex, what is it?"

"It's not just that guy, Kelsey. There are more here."

She looked around, confused. "More what?"

"More people."

"I don't think so."

"Come with me. I'll show you." He held out his hand and she glared at him, refusing to allow him to touch her again. With a shrug, he walked toward the clearing. Unable to resist, she followed.

The man who'd been waiting for him turned around. She recognized him. It was Brandon King, one of Jason's staffers. But he was the only other person in the park. So what did Jason mean by more people?

When they reached the center of the clearing, Jason stepped toward her, taking her by her upper arms and forcing her to meet his gaze. "Listen to me Kelsey. What you're going to see will shock you. You won't believe it at first, and then it will frighten you. Don't be afraid. No harm will come to you as long as you stay by my side."

His words confused her even more. What the hell was he talking about?

Oh good God. He wasn't part of some satanic cult, was he? Her mind whirled with the possibilities. Some kind of secret organization? Hell, what if he was affiliated with terrorists? Could her feelings have been all wrong about Jason? What if he wasn't the man she'd thought he was?

No. She refused to believe it.

Out of the corner of her eye, she spotted more people entering the clearing. Startled, she sucked in a breath. Where had they been hiding? She hadn't heard or seen them. And yet there had to be over a hundred of them filling the clearing. From young adults to older folks, men and women. She spotted the blonde bimbo from the hotel the other night! They came nearer and nearer to Jason and to her. She found herself sidling closer to Jason, feeling more uncomfortable and claustrophobic as the crowd surrounded them.

Jason grabbed her hand and said something in a language she didn't understand. She turned to him, and then he shouted the words in English as he looked at her.

"This is *mine*!"

He meant her. Dammit, he meant her. What did he mean by that? She wasn't his.

Then a low growl caught her attention and she turned to the crowd. They were snarling at her, their eyes glowing an eerie yellow.

Glowing? She blinked, certain the moon played tricks on her. But when she turned to Jason, his eyes had taken on a golden hue, just as the others.

"Don't be afraid, Kelsey," he said, his voice thicker than it had been before. And he had...hair on his face. Hair that was growing rapidly.

She had to be hallucinating. Sharp cries filled the night air as painful moans and howls surrounded her. Clothes were discarded and bodies sprouted fur. Everyone around her was changing, including Jason!

Chapter Seven

Jason swore under his breath, his body warring with the unavoidable change and his desire to remain human.

Dammit, this wasn't the way he'd wanted to reveal himself to Kelsey. Not during a pack fest. Not when he could barely control them all during the full moon. As it was, he'd have to count on his closest allies to make sure things didn't get out of hand. He had to keep Kelsey safe, and the only way he knew to do that was in wolf form. Or at least partial wolf form. Then, he'd have the strength to fight off any challengers. If he stayed human and they all changed, they might be able to take him down.

Now that he'd staked his claim on Kelsey, he expected challengers. There were a handful of pack members who felt he shouldn't lead them. He hadn't led them very long, so until he firmly established himself as the dominant male, he knew he'd be challenged. During full moon, he always had to defend his right to be alpha.

He'd win, of course, but he'd have to take care of Kelsey too.

Kelsey, who right now regarded him with fear and loathing. Her eyes were wide with horror as she began to back away. She'd no more take a few steps then she'd bump into a changing wolf and scurry forward again.

He had to be in the center of the pack. It was the only way to assert his control. And she had to stay with him.

"Kelsey. Don't run. Stay with me. It's the only way you'll be safe."

"Safe? You call this safe? What the fuck is happening here, Jason?"

Her high-pitched voice told him she was nearly hysterical. He could only imagine what this must be like viewed from a human's eyes. Changing from human to wolf was messy, the sounds of bones shifting and reforming in different positions, muscles expanding and growing thicker, hair spurting out all over. Snarling, growling, elongating of teeth and salivating.

"We're werewolves, Kelsey. And there are more of us than you think. We come from all different backgrounds and locations. We don't hunt and kill like you see in the movies. When in human form, we're just like everyone else. But we are dominant in wolf form."

"You don't even look like a regular wolf. You're still standing, but you look...strange."

"We take many forms. Human, half-wolf as I am right now, and we can also take on the full wolf form. In this way, I can still speak to you. In full wolf form I can't."

"You have an erection." He watched her eyes widen as she focused between his legs. Her gaze only made his cock stand out more prominently.

The change was an erotic experience for a werewolf. During the monthly pack meet there would be sex of every kind imaginable. Sounds of lustful howling would sail through the night, going on until right before dawn.

He hadn't wanted to expose Kelsey to all this yet, but now he had no choice. The best he could do would be to control his own lustful urges. Right now, his blood boiled with the primal urge to take her, throw her to the ground and drive his cock deep into her until she begged for mercy. The need to mate was strong, the lust nearly overpowering. His cock rose between his legs, longer and thicker now than it was in human form. His balls were tight and hot, aching with the need for release.

But he was stronger than the beast. He had to be. Kelsey's very life could depend on it. "I won't lie to you, Kelsey. The need to fuck you right now is very strong. But if I take you in this form, I will brand you and make you lupine. Once you are turned, you will be like me."

She stepped back and raised her hands in front of her. "Don't touch me. Don't ever touch me again."

His heart sank at the revulsion on her face. She wouldn't accept him. Others would know it and would challenge him for her. He didn't want to use force on her, but he had no choice. He reached for her and clasped his hand around her wrist, careful not to scratch her with his claws. His strength in this form was more than enough to keep her next to him.

"Listen carefully. Don't move. Don't try to get away. I am alpha of this pack, which means I'm their leader. I've claimed you as my mate. If you deny that claim in front of them, it makes you fair game for a challenge by those who seek to take over as alpha. They'll run after you. They'll catch you. And when they do, they'll fuck you until you bleed and scream for mercy."

"No. You're saying that to scare me."

"Look around you. I wish I was just trying to scare you, but it's the truth." He held tight to her wrist and drew her against his chest. "I am no different now than I was before. I'm still the man who loves you."

Her fingers curled against her palm. "Don't say that. It's a lie!"

"Don't raise your voice to me!" He hated to sound so harsh, but it was imperative the pack not see how she felt. "You can hate me later. Right now, you need to act as if you want to be by my side. I need to touch you, to stake my claim on you in front of everyone. I won't fuck you, but I'm going to come damn close to it. Trust me on this. If you don't, you could die tonight."

Kelsey fought the emotions warring inside her. She didn't know what to do. Shock made coherent thought impossible. She wanted to be revolted by Jason's appearance. He looked so different, with his glowing eyes and facial hair, his chest huge and barrel-like and his cock so goddamn big she wanted to faint.

Lust filled her. Her panties were soaked, her body on fire as if some strange spell had been cast on her.

Hell, maybe it had.

She didn't want to desire Jason. Not like this. Not now that she knew what he was. And yet, she couldn't help herself. She was still drawn to him.

Somewhere deep inside, past the hurt and anger, she knew he told her the truth. If she didn't do exactly as he said, the others would take her. She glanced around at the half-dozen males sniffing the air around her, their faces more like a wolves than men. They were so close she could reach out and touch them. They licked their long teeth, their eyes glowing as they kept their focus on her and her alone.

She had to trust Jason. She stepped into his arms, winding her fingers into the thick pelt on his chest. "I hate this. I want you to know I hate this. And I hate you."

He hissed but nodded. "Fine. Hate me. I just want to get you out of this alive, so just go along with me. And for God's sake, at least pretend you're enjoying it."

That wouldn't be a problem. Her body screamed for his touch, his tongue, his cock. She wanted him to possess her. Hell, she wanted him to fuck her, right in front of this crowd. She might hate him, but she wanted him.

"Undress," he commanded. "And be quick about it or I'll tear your clothes off."

Before she could think about what she was doing, she stripped off her shoes and clothes and stood there naked, feeling more exposed and vulnerable than she'd ever felt before. Even though everyone else was naked, they at least had fur covering parts of their bodies.

Jason turned her around so her back was to him. He ran his hands over her breasts, her traitorous nipples responding to the scrape of his palms. He cupped her, and she noticed he didn't touch her with his long claws. Moving his hands down over her abdomen, he brushed her sex with two long fingers. Her legs trembled and he wrapped his free arm around her middle to hold her steady.

"I could sink my teeth into the nape of your neck right now and fuck you, Kelsey. Do you know how much I want my cock inside you?"

She wondered if he had any idea how much she wanted the same thing.

"But if I take your pussy and shoot my come into your womb, you become lupine. I won't do that to you without your consent."

She was grateful for that, at least.

As he stroked her moist slit and flicked his thumb over her clit, he whispered harshly in her ear. "But if I take your ass, you stay human."

Oh God. Her pussy quaked at the thought of that huge cock buried in her ass. She wanted to scream "No!" as loud as she could. But she didn't. She wanted to think the reason she didn't was to protect herself. But that wasn't true. The real reason was because she wanted him to fuck her that way.

This would be the last time she'd be with him. Damn her soul to hell, she wanted him to fuck her! "Take me that way, Jason. Take my ass."

His hot breath sailed across her cheeks as his tongue snaked out and licked her neck. His rumbling growl reverberated against her back. "Get down on your knees."

She did as he commanded, nearly falling to the soft ground. Jason covered her immediately, snarling at the other wolves who hovered nearby. "This bitch is mine!" he said in a voice that didn't sound like him. "Watch me fuck her."

They were all going to watch. Their cocks jutted out from their hairy bodies, glistening with drops of pre-come. Heaven help her, but the sight of their shafts only added to her excitement. The thought that Jason's possession of her would be witnessed by all of them, while they could do nothing but stand by and watch, nearly had her climaxing on the spot.

She heard Jason's sniffing noises behind her as he moved down her back, licking and scraping his teeth lightly against her skin. She moaned when he moved his mouth between her legs and licked her nectar, then wound his tongue around her clit and lapped her until she whimpered. He snaked his tongue into the crevice of her buttocks, licking the puckered hole until sparks of lightning-like pleasure shot to her pussy.

When she thought she couldn't bear it any longer, he moved over her back, positioning his cock between her buttocks. He probed the small entrance with the head and slid partway in.

She stilled, waiting for him to plunge in hard and deep. But he was gentle, taking it inch by inch until he pushed past the tight barrier, then thrust all the way inside her.

Unable to contain her cries, she let them out, tears rolling down her cheeks at the pleasurable pain of being so filled by Jason's cock. He moved back, then drove harder. Instinctively she reached for her clit and massaged the ache that was making her mad.

"Fuck your pussy for me, Kelsey," he said, his voice straining. She knew he held back for her, because he didn't want to hurt her. As she slipped two fingers into her dripping cunt, she no longer wanted safety or a gentle touch.

"Give it to me, Jason. Fuck my ass hard."

He snarled and grabbed her neck with his teeth, holding her in place as he reared back and drove deep. Sliding her fingers into her pussy, she matched his tempo as he pounded his cock in her ass. When she felt the first strains of her orgasm approach, she cried out into the already lust-filled night and dove over the edge, taking Jason with her.

His howls rent the night air. The others watched him climax. His hot seed filled her ass, pouring down her legs and over her pussy. She took his cream and rubbed it over her still-spasming clit. Jason collapsed over her back, panting as hard as she was.

She felt as if she were in a dream-like state, unable to even focus on the others any longer, not caring what happened to them, or to herself. She was exhausted, mentally and physically. Jason picked her up and carried her back to the house. She felt safe cradled in his strong arms and snuggled closer to his warmth.

When they returned, he bathed her, then gently tucked her into his bed and pulled up a chair next to her. The last things she saw were dawn breaking over the tops of the trees and Jason's silhouette as he continued to sit next to her and stroke her hair.

Then she gave up and closed her eyes, letting the bliss of sleep overtake her.

* * * * *

Kelsey sat in front of the laptop, staring at a blank page.

After what happened last night, Jason had let her sleep. When she woke, she dressed while he waited silently, then made arrangements for his limo to take her home. Before she walked out the door, he reached for her hand.

"I never meant for this to happen. I won't apologize for who and what I am, because I was born this way. But you have all the choices here. What you decide to do with the information you have is up to you. What you choose to do with the fact that I love you is also up to you."

She'd walked away without giving him an answer, because frankly, she didn't know what to do.

She loved him. But she loved Jason the man, not Jason the werewolf.

Didn't she? Right now she was having a hard time separating the two.

This whole thing was simply too bizarre to comprehend. She had what amounted to the story of the century. Revealing the fact that werewolves were not the subject of folklore and cinema, but in fact lived among humans, had to be a Pulitzer Prize winning story in the making

She'd be rich. And famous.

And Jason would be ruined. No doubt hunted down and used for research. And what of the others? The ones who looked like normal people before they changed. People she ran into at the grocery story or at work. Hell, she could work with some of them for all she knew.

Frustrated, she closed the laptop and paced her apartment, her mind no clearer now than it had been when the limo had brought her home.

What would happen if she exposed Jason and the others? She would be responsible for not only the downfall of his political career, but no doubt the rounding up and persecution of his entire family.

Face it, Kelsey. The world just isn't ready for people who fall outside the norm.

The man she loved was a werewolf. But he was also a wonderful senator, a passionate man and she was crazy in love with him.

She knew what she had to do.

* * * * *

Jason refused to get the newspaper. It had been two days since Kelsey had left his house. No one had arrived yesterday morning to take him away. No reporters hounded him for proof that he was a werewolf.

Maybe she'd needed a day to get it together and it would be in this morning's paper. How could she walk away from a story like this?

He stared down into his coffee, hoping the black brew would provide the answers he sought. When the doorbell rang, he jumped and glanced at the clock.

Christ, it was five a.m. Dread filled him. The newspapers were out now. He felt incredible sorrow for what was about to happen to his family, to the people who'd loved him and protected the family secret for centuries. He'd let them down. He'd ruined them.

With a sigh, he rose from the table and went to face his accusers.

But when he opened the door, there were no reporters.

Just Kelsey, holding out his morning paper. "It's a little wet. Your sprinklers just came on."

He took it from her hands, too dumbfounded to even speak.

"You gonna let me in?"

"Yeah. Sorry." He watched her walk into the kitchen and grab a cup, pouring herself some coffee and sliding into a chair.

"Mmm, I needed this," she said, holding the cup with both hands.

"Kelsey, why are you here?"

"I have questions. Lots of them."

"Okay." What did that mean? That she was going to wait to write her story until she got more details?

"Like what it means when I become lupine. And pups. Do we really have pups or will our kids be human?"

"Huh?"

"Jason! Wake up! I have too many questions for you to have your head in the clouds."

"Did you just say 'when' you become lupine?" He had to be dreaming this.

"Yes. And don't forget the part about pups. That I really want to know about because I love kids."

"Me too." He stepped toward her and kneeled, almost afraid to touch her in case she was an hallucination. "I love you, Kelsey."

He didn't misread the warmth in her eyes. "I love you too, Jason. Werewolf or not, I can't live without you."

His heart nearly burst from his chest at the realization that she was not only going to keep his secret, but that she wanted to be with him. He stood and pulled her up, then kissed her with all the love he felt. And what he received in return convinced him that he'd made the right choice in his mate.

Her eyes had darkened and her lips curled into a sexy smile. "Now, about my questions."

"Later. Right now, I need to properly propose to you. In bed." He swooped her into his arms and took the stairs two at a time.

"Someday, Jason, I'm going to write this story," she said as he laid her on the bed and began to peel her clothes off.

"Someday Kelsey, we'll *want* the world to know all about it."

But not today. Today, it was enough that she knew, that she accepted, and that she loved him.

About the author:

Jaci Burton has been a dreamer and lover of romance her entire life. Consumed with stories of passion, love and happily ever afters, she finally pulled her fantasy characters out of her head and put them on paper. Writing allows her to showcase the rainbow of emotions that result from falling in love. Jaci lives in Oklahoma with her husband (her fiercest writing critic and sexy inspiration), stepdaughter and three wild and crazy dogs. Her sons are grown and live on opposite coasts and don't bother her nearly as often as she'd like them to. When she isn't writing stories of passion and romance, she can usually be found at the gym, reading a great book, or working on her computer, trying to figure out how she can pull more than twenty-four hours out of a single day.

Jaci welcomes mail from readers. You can write to her c/o Ellora's Cave Publishing at 1337 Commerce Drive, Suite 13, Stow OH 44224.

Also by Jaci Burton:

WOLFE'S HOPE

Lora Leigh

Prologue

July 1996, Genetics Council, Wolf Breed Labs
Mexico

Wolfe growled in fury, his teeth bared, his body taut, ready to spring as they pushed the young woman into his cell once again. She carried his scent now, proof that she was his mate. The mark he had given her the day before was still vividly evident on her upper shoulder.

"You'll do as I demand this time, Wolfe, or Hope will take the beating instead of you," Delia Bainesmith told him coldly.

"She's your daughter," he howled out in fury. "How can you do this to her?"

"She is a lab rat, no more, no less than are you," she informed him smugly. "Now breed her. She's ovulating, and we've made certain she's ready. Fuck her, my little wolf, or she'll be the one who pays."

The Bitch walked away, her laughter echoing behind her as Hope whimpered in sexual distress. They had given her an aphrodisiac, ensuring she would accept him.

"Please, Wolfe." Her slender body shook with tremors of arousal. "It hurts."

"I can't, Hope." He couldn't look at her. "I won't."

She was just a child, barely seventeen. He wouldn't scar her, either physically or emotionally, with what he knew was coming.

"She'll beat me," she whispered.

"She won't get the chance." He knew that.

"She said you mated with me. How did you mate with me, without taking me?"

He could almost hear the tears whispering over her pale cheeks.

"I marked you, Hope." He couldn't stop his eyes from going to the proof of his ownership. "No other will touch you. No other will have you. That mark and the scent it places on you is mine alone. Don't make the mistake of ever allowing another man in your bed. Because I'll kill him."

Cold, hard rage shuddered through him at the thought. He had killed one soldier already over her. The one who had dared to fondle her breasts as they tore her clothes from her the day before.

"I'm sorry she did this. It's my fault, for loving you." As always, she would try to take the blame on her slender shoulders.

"No, Hope, it is my fault," he told her bleakly. "Mine for ever desiring to hope for more."

* * * * *

Explosions ripped through the compound. Gunfire exploded around the small house into which Hope was locked; the smell of burning buildings, the sounds of horrified screams echoed in her head.

"Wolfe!" She screamed out his name. Huddled in the bedroom on the opposite end of the house, terrified it would go up in flames at any minute, she prayed he would find her.

The ground rocked and plaster showered from the roof as she pressed herself closer to the huge dresser that she prayed would deflect the ceiling should it fall. She screamed out Wolfe's name again. He would come for her soon.

The sound of the front door slamming had her on her feet, racing for the doorway. Her abrupt halt just inside the living room had her rocking on her heels. Her mother stood there, furious, shaking, her normally austere composure crumpled.

"Wolfe," Hope couldn't stop her cry, her unasked question.

"The son of a bitch is dead. They all are," she sneered. "They hit the labs first, and it's an inferno. Forget it, Hope, save yourself now. Don't worry about that mongrel excuse for a man."

Hope slid to the floor, the wall supporting her body, her mind unable to accept, unable to process the meaning of her mother's words.

"He'll come for me," she whispered.

Cruelty echoed in Delia Bainesmith's demented laughter.

"Wishful thinking, daughter. That bastard will never cum again. Too bad. You might have enjoyed it."

Chapter One
Six Years Later, July 2002
Albuquerque, New Mexico

Hope Bainesmith knew when she received the phone call from her mother that it wasn't going to be a good day. The woman hadn't bothered to call her for years, had taken no interest in her life other than the monthly medical tests Hope was required to take. So the phone call that morning had caused her no small amount of concern.

"Have you seen Wolfe?" Hope's knees had weakened at the question. She collapsed into the kitchen chair, stilling the pain that raged in her chest.

Wolfe. Her hand touched the mark at her upper shoulder. Her body throbbed in remembrance. It was that mark that made the monthly tests necessary. An odd quirk of nature, given to a man that was created by science. The small bite had allowed a minute amount of an unknown hormone into her blood. It marked her pheromones and acted as a very mild aphrodisiac. She had been in arousal hell ever since. Hence the reason for monthly medicals.

"Wolfe's dead, mother. Remember?" she reminded the creature who spawned her. "How could I see him?"

There was silence over the line. Hope knew her voice reflected the grief she still lived with on a daily basis. It had been nearly six years but she could still remember with brutal clarity the attack on the labs, the engulfing blaze and the horrendous screams from those trapped inside.

"We never recovered a body," Dr. Bainesmith reminded her, her cultured voice cool and autocratic.

Hope could just see her petite, pretty mother, her black eyes as cold as ice, her Asian features a cool mask of studied indifference. Nothing mattered but the project at hand, and nothing else would matter. But Wolfe wasn't a project anymore, she wanted to scream, and neither was she.

"There were a lot of bodies you didn't recover," Hope pointed out painfully. "Wolfe's dead, let him rest in peace now."

She hung up the phone carefully, fighting the tears that filled her eyes. The instinctive longing welled inside her at the oddest times. Wolfe was dead. No amount of grieving could bring him back. There was no justice to be found—no matter what she did—in his death.

Her mother refused to accept it. Wolfe was *her* creation; she considered him and his Pack *her* property. He had defeated her with his death, and Hope knew the other woman could not accept that she would no longer command the army she had envisioned. A pack of savage soldiers with the instincts and intelligence of an animal.

The world was still in shock, even now, years after the broadcast of the first Breeds, felines in that case, announcing their lives. Those men and women, created by science, had been genetically altered with the DNA of savage cats. They had been created to kill. "Disposable soldiers," one announcer had reported. The Breeds they were called, for want of a better name. It was during the broadcast of that announcement that the labs in Mexico had been raided by Mexican and American agents. It had been a brutal, bloody battle, one that would have done any drug lord proud. But it wasn't drugs they sought; it was the human experimentations and the scientists and soldiers who made their lives hell that the agents wanted.

Hope shuddered at the memories of screams, the erupting flames and gunfire echoing around the house in which she hid. She had screamed Wolfe's name over and over during those hours. Certain he would have escaped. But had he escaped, he would surely have come for her. He had claimed her, swore she belonged to him. He wouldn't have left her there to die.

Sighing deeply, she collected her jacket and backpack and headed for class. Her day was full, her life was heading somewhere for a change. She couldn't allow the memories to destroy all she had gained in the past years.

Exiting her small apartment, she noticed the white cleaner's van in the parking lot, but paid it little heed. She noticed the large men moving about outside its opened doors, but the sight was a common one. What she wasn't expecting was the hard grip one of them took of her arm as she passed. For a brief second surprise flared in Hope's chest as one of the tall men stepped before her, a growl emitting from his lips, his gray eyes swirling with anger. She gasped, then blinked as something stung her arm.

"Wolfe," she whispered his name in desperation as she felt the shocking, abrupt departure of consciousness.

Chapter Two

Hope awoke disoriented, groggy. She blinked up at the ceiling and stared at the heavy beams that crossed it. This wasn't her bedroom. She looked around, taking careful stock of the large room. The heavy logs that made up the walls told her she was in a cabin. The scent of a fire burning, the low hum of voices assured her she wasn't alone. She shifted against the mattress, intending to rise from the bed and demand a heated explanation. Fury flared in her as she tried to move but couldn't.

Her legs and arms were tied to the four corners of the bed like a damned virginal sacrifice. She was still dressed, but only barely. Her shirt had been unbuttoned to the waist, her jeans unsnapped, the zipper lowered. Her body hummed with arousal, ached in ways it hadn't for years. *Wolfe.* Only his touch, only the stroke of his tongue, the caress of his lips could put her into such burning arousal.

He had touched her. She stifled a sob, closing her eyes as she let the knowledge soak into her brain. He was alive, and he had dared to touch her while she was unconscious. Her eyes flew open again. The tips of her breasts were so sensitive she could swear that just breathing irritated them. Her abdomen was heated, a spot on her hip sang with sensation. Her blood pulsed through her veins. A rapid tattoo of lust had her shifting against her bonds, trying to clench her thighs to relieve the ache that centered in her very womb.

He had touched her with his mouth, tasted her. She almost whimpered. She held the sound back though, knowing well his exceptional hearing. He would know she was awake, and he would come to her. Tears stung her eyes. He was alive, all these years he had been alive and he had never come to her. Had not contacted her. He had left her *suffering*. Her lips thinned, her eyes narrowed. Damn him, he knew what he had done to her the night her mother had locked her in his cell. He knew he had marked her as his mate, ensuring that no other male, normal or Wolf Breed, would take her with her cooperation.

She still carried the scar of that mark on her shoulder. A sharp bite, then gentle strokes of the tongue that infected the area with a hormone so potent that it took very little, and no time at all for it to make its way to the bloodstream.

She had been in misery that night, so hot, needing him so desperately that she had pleaded with him for hours. But that one touch, that one caress was all he allowed her, and he had been furious with himself, and with her, when he realized what he had done.

Of course, the Bitch had been overjoyed, certain that it would be only a matter of time before Wolfe proved her theory that the Breed's DNA would in fact find a way to procreate. Their females were barren. There was enough evidence to support the theory that the mutated sperm the males carried would change once again to ensure breeding. Her daughter had been chosen as the first lab rat for the procedure.

Hope had never cared much for the cold, sarcastic woman that she knew as her mother. But when she had learned the calculated plan to use her so coldly, she had begun to hate her.

"I see you're awake." Her eyes flew open as his cool, dark voice greeted her from the open doorway.

He was older, but still so handsome he took her breath away. His hair was black, cut shorter in the front and tapering down below his neck, brushing his shoulders. He wore a blue cotton shirt tucked into jeans and a wide belt cinched at his hips. Below, the fabric bulged with the pressure of his erection.

Hope swallowed with no small amount of difficulty. He was more intimidating than ever before. But he was alive. So alive he took her breath with his presence.

"You tied me up. You touched me while I was unconscious," she accused him, suddenly furious he had allowed her to be tormented for six long years. "You're no better than the bastards who created you, Wolfe."

The words, born of hurt and fury, could not be taken back, and she had no desire to do so. How dare he leave her hurting, aching all these years? How dare he kidnap her and frighten her, rather than coming to her as he should have?

She watched in shock though, as complete fury filled the thundercloud color of his eyes.

"And you, my sweet sacrifice, are no better than the bitch that bore you," he sneered. "Do you think I wanted to be recaptured, forced to breed and see my children raised as I was? Did you honestly believe the plan the two of you hatched would come to fruition?"

Hope stared up at him in confusion. How could he believe she would plan anything with her mother when she hadn't even known he was alive?

"What plan?" she asked. "I made no plan with her."

His lips twisted in a sneer as he entered the room, closing the door behind him. God, she was burning alive for him. She could barely think for the need to touch him, to be touched by him, now that he was close to her. His very presence caused sharp pangs of lust to ripple through her pussy.

"You won't lie to me for long, Hope," he told her softly, his gray eyes going over her body as they darkened with lust. "I promise, before this night ends you'll beg to tell me the truth."

The sensual promise in his voice made her breath catch. His hands went to his belt, releasing the catch with slow, measured movements. Her eyes widened as he began to pull it from the loops. She began to wonder if he had something in mind for her rather than the fucking she needed so desperately.

"You wouldn't dare beat me," she finally gasped.

He dropped the belt to the floor, smiling in amusement as his fingers then went to the buttons on his shirt. Hope trembled. She could feel her cunt heating further, the muscles of her vagina clenching in preparation. Her heart sped up, beating a harsh, driving pulse against her breast.

"I may spank you, but I promise not to beat you," he said, his rough voice silky, brooding. "But you can halt any punishment at all, Hope, by telling me the truth. Tell me how she knew of the mating frenzy, and how she knew you would be the one I would choose as my mate. Tell me why you allowed another man to touch you, allowed her to taunt me with the proof of it."

"Are you crazy?" she practically yelled at him. "How the hell am I supposed to let another man touch me when all I do is puke if they try?"

That infuriated her more than anything else. The few times she had tried to date, tried to get over him, had turned into a disaster within an hour.

"So innocent and outraged." His smile sent a shiver up her spine, but did little to alleviate the need in her cunt. "One last chance, tell me how that bitch mother of yours knew we had not perished in that fire?"

Her need for him was making her crazy. If he didn't fuck her soon, she would be a screaming idiot. She had waited long enough — six torturous years dreaming of him, aching for him.

Hope blinked up at him. He was shrugging out of the shirt, his broad, muscular chest gleaming in the dim light of the bedroom. His muscles rippled, tightened. His face was tense as his fingers fell to the snap of his jeans.

"I don't know," she whispered.

She couldn't take her eyes off his movements. He would shed his jeans next, revealing the extent of his arousal. She remembered well how thick and long it was, a temptation even to the teenager she had been so long ago.

The scientists had kept them naked. She remembered watching Wolfe move about the compound, unashamed of his nakedness, even during arousal. So tall and broad, he moved with an innate grace that had drawn her attention time and again.

His hands hooked into the waist of the material as he kicked his feet free of whatever shoes he was wearing. Within seconds, he was gloriously naked. His cock rose to his abdomen, tight, hard, thick and engorged. The bulbous head was purplish, flaring just a bit thicker than the shaft, and throbbing with arousal.

"Oh, God," she whispered breathlessly.

He moved to the bed, kneeling beside her, staring down at her with a cold, hard expression. He meant to be a bastard, she knew, but she could see the heat licking in the dark shadows of his eyes. He wasn't unaffected, and the engorged cock wasn't his only reaction to her. She was his mate, and whatever he did, she knew he wouldn't hurt her. At least, not physically.

Chapter Three

For a moment, his expression softened.

"Do you know how long I have waited to touch you as I want to?" he growled, his voice harsh as his hands went to her shirt to finish unbuttoning it. "Do you have any idea how hard it was to maintain my control before, and not take the innocence of the child you were?"

Hope felt herself trembling, her flesh sensitizing as she felt the heat of his hands, the hard promise of his body.

"I offered," she whispered. No, she hadn't, she had begged. She had cried and pleaded with him to take her after he left that mark on her upper shoulder.

"And so you did," he agreed, his voice lethal, his eyes swirling with anger as he stared down at her. "I wanted only to protect you, Hope. How did you repay the sacrifice I made to ensure that protection?"

His hand circled her neck. He applied no pressure, but she knew he wanted her to know that the threat was there. All she could feel was the fire of longing, though. It zipped through her veins, bubbled in her cunt.

"What did I do?" She shook her head, seeing rage in his eyes, rage and lust and a spark of pain. "I didn't do anything, Wolfe."

She couldn't understand the rage she glimpsed in him as she denied betraying him. How could she betray him? Even her soul knew she belonged to Wolfe.

"You betrayed me with another man," he snarled. "Don't bother to lie to me, woman. You have lain beneath others. Took them into your body and let them fuck you rather than waiting for me to come to you."

Hope felt the blood drain from her face.

"That's not true," she gasped, horrified. How could he believe such a thing? "I swear it's not, Wolfe. I've never been with another man."

He shook his head with a sharp negative movement. His lips twisted with bitterness, with bleak fury.

"You would think I could still smell the betrayal on your body, the scent of another's seed. I am so captivated by your beauty, by my own need, I can't even smell the traitorous scent." He seemed angrier with himself now, as though his senses refused to see what was there, merely because he did not want to believe it.

"Because there is none," she said, furious. "What do you have to do, rape me to figure it out? Damn you, I'm still a virgin. It wouldn't take a rocket scientist to figure it out."

She knew well his possessive instincts. After his refusal to take her, her mother had taunted him outside the cell. Two of the Lab's soldiers had held her, fondling her as Wolfe was forced to watch.

Wolfe had sat in the cell; cold, hard, the shifting colors in his eyes dangerously alive. Her mother had finally relented and had Hope released. After Hope was thrown back in the cell with him once again, she stalked away from them.

Wolfe had held her, comforted her, but still refused to take her. The next time he was released from the cell, the two soldiers who touched her had died.

"You are no longer a virgin, Hope," he finally said heavily, his expression filled with disgust. "How do you even hope to convince me of such a lie?"

His gray eyes glittered with anger. He stared down at her as though she had just informed him that he had mistaken her for someone else. She shook her head, anger building inside her.

"How can you say that? Do you think that just because you forgot so easily about me, that I could do the same thing? Too bad I couldn't mark you as well. Maybe then you wouldn't have forgotten so easily."

"And you think you did not?" he growled. "I have the proof of your betrayal, Hope. The pictures the Bitch sent me of you trapped between their bodies, your face twisted with pleasure."

The possessive rage was thick, dangerous. His body was tight with it, his eyes glowing in fury.

"Pictures can be faked," she threw back at him furiously. "I am still a virgin, the proof is there—"

"And do you think I did not check that first thing?" he asked her coldly. "Do you think I am such a fool I would not know if the obstruction was there or not? I have checked, Hope, and there is none. You can stop lying this moment."

Hope stilled. She stared up at him, uncomprehending. His rage was a tangible thing, and yet so was his pain.

"What do you mean?" she whispered in confusion. "It's there."

He shook his head, a snarl of fury on his lips, though his voice stayed level this time.

"Why do you think your pants are open? Why do you think the demand of your body is so much worse than before? I checked. I slid my finger easily inside you, Hope, deep inside. Your sweet pussy gripped me tighter than a glove, but there was no obstruction. You are no virgin. Did you not think I would check to be certain? Do you think I would not give my mate the benefit of a doubt where that bitch's claims are concerned? I beg you to cease your lies. Tell me what I want to know, now."

And Wolfe wouldn't lie. Of course, he would have checked first. He never made claims he wasn't certain of. He was coldly logical, always in control of himself and his facts. It had been one of the things that drove her mother insane at the labs. How easily he could show her for the vicious, incompetent monster she was. She had lost nearly all support for her control of the labs within the Genetic Council that backed it, before the raid had taken it apart.

"You made a mistake." There was no other explanation, though she feared there was.

She felt tears gather behind her eyes. She wouldn't shed them, not now where he could see and would ridicule them. Pain bloomed in her heart, in her soul. She knew as sure as she lived that if what Wolfe said was true, then her mother had somehow arranged for the hymen to be broken during her last visit to the doctor. She remembered being more tender than usual, more uncomfortable during the physical exam than she normally was.

Her scream of denial was a silent one. She stilled, fighting to breathe, to get through the pain one second at a time. That was all she could do.

"There is no mistake." He punctuated his words by ripping the shirt from her arms then tossing the tattered remains to the floor.

After the first flinch, Hope merely lay still, staring up at him. He was so coldly furious, enraged at what he saw as her deception. It wouldn't matter if she had found a way to be with another man, she wouldn't have done so. Wolfe held her heart and soul.

Her breath hitched in her throat as he stared down at her now. She wanted so desperately to allow her tears to fall, but she couldn't. Not yet. Not now. Later, when he no longer watched her, when she could no longer see the cold detachment in his eyes.

"Did you bring me more clothes?" She kept her voice even, cool. She couldn't lose control now. She wouldn't.

He narrowed his eyes on her.

"You will need no clothes until you tell me the plans the Bitch has made for me and my Pack and how damaging the information is that she has on our whereabouts," he told her, his voice hateful, cold and hard.

Hope swallowed past the knot of betrayal in her throat.

"I don't know any of her plans," she whispered. "I didn't even know you were alive until you kidnapped me. She hasn't spoken your name in all these years until she called this morning and asked if I had seen you."

"Wrong answer." He lifted a knife from the bedside table and cut her bra away. "Try again."

Hope was silent. She stared up at the ceiling, fighting to breathe through her pain as he cut her jeans and panties from her body next. She had no clothes now, no pride.

She prayed for detachment, but when his hand cupped her between her legs, two fingers burying into her damp slit, she was unable to stop her needy cry or the arch of her body.

"Your pussy is so wet, so slick for me," he growled. "Tell me, sweet Hope, did you get this wet for the men who have fucked you since I marked you as my own?"

His voice was rough and angry, but his touch was gentle, arousing. She felt her juices flow over his fingers, her cunt contracting painfully with the need for release.

"There have been no other men," she said, fighting to breathe through the intense sensations whipping through her body. "I swear it, Wolfe."

His fingers parted the folds of her cunt, then she felt a wailing cry shatter her body as the two fingers slid deep and easily into her vagina. They stretched her, filled her, making her hungry cunt clasp them desperately. But there was no obstruction.

Chapter Four

"Where is your virginity, Hope?" He was lodged deep inside her now, and he had met no resistance. "I will not punish you for the betrayal of your body. I know the games that bitch mother of yours plays. But if you do not tell me how she plans to strike against the Pack, then I will punish you, and I will not stop until you give me what I want." He pulled back, then thrust inside her firmly once again.

Hope lost her breath. It was such near bliss. Pleasure arced over her body, through it; lightning heated her skin as she strained toward the building pressure centered at his tormenting fingers.

"I swear to you, Wolfe. I swear, she hasn't told me anything," Hope panted, her head twisting on the pillows, her hips fighting to drive his fingers inside her again.

"How can I believe you, beloved?" he questioned her gently. "You will not even admit to the loss of your virginity. Lies spill from your lips like honeyed caresses on a heated night."

A tear spilled from her eye. She stared resolutely at the ceiling above her, fighting her pleas, but she couldn't still her body as easily. Her hips jerked as his fingers thrust slowly inside her cunt once again. The biting pleasure/pain from the smooth thrust was like fiery fingers of near ecstasy. Damn him, he knew what he was doing; she could hear it in his controlled breathing, feel it in the tormenting thrusts inside her.

"I'm not your beloved." She shook her head, fighting not to beg. "I'm nothing to you."

Silence greeted her words. His fingers stilled inside her, then slid free.

"Why would you say such a thing?" he asked her harshly, angrily.

Hope glanced at him in surprise. He was frowning down at her, his expression dark, confused at her feelings, as though his actions spoke differently. As though he were loving her rather than punishing her. Not that her body knew the difference right at that moment.

"How could I believe otherwise," she whispered. "I'm supposedly your mate, but when those fires swept through the compound, you didn't come for me. Afterward, you never gave me so much as a sign that you lived. I was nothing to you, Wolfe, until you thought I had something you needed. Until you couldn't stay away from me any longer."

And that hurt most of all. She had spent six years in pain, physical as well as emotional. Her nightmares were those of the months she was with him at the lab. Seeing him beaten, seeing her mother take pleasure in marring his body, ridiculing the honor that was such a part of him. It had infuriated the doctor that he refused to rape the women brought to him for breeding. That he would not perform for her sadistic pleasures. But what enraged her mother more thoroughly was the fact that she couldn't break him, no matter how hard she tried.

"Why?" she asked him desperately. "Why didn't you come for me, Wolfe?"

He didn't speak; rather he trailed his moist fingers from her cunt, along her abdomen, then ringed her hardened nipples with the juices from her body. Hope felt her face flush as he watched her. Her nipples were throbbing for attention now. Her clit felt swollen, desperate; she could barely breath she was so aroused.

"You are all that truly matters to me," he whispered regretfully, his gaze meeting hers hesitantly. "Since you were seventeen years old, staring up at me with big, innocent blue eyes, you have been my world."

Her throat tightened in pain. He sounded so sincere, so deeply honest that she wanted nothing more than to believe in him. And she knew suddenly that it was how he felt as well. He wanted to believe, but the lies her mother had set in motion made that impossible.

"Then why didn't you come for me?" she asked, then cried out in such sensual arousal she felt faint as he brought his fingers to his mouth, tasting her juices with a growl of hungry need.

"Your taste makes me hungry for more, sweet Hope," he told her, his voice dark, throbbing with sexual intensity.

"Wolfe, I'll beg you, if that's what you want," she whimpered. "Please don't do this to me. Fuck me and get it over with, or don't touch me. Please. I swear to you, you're making a mistake."

He gripped a nipple between his thumb and forefinger. Hope couldn't contain the cry of pleasure that swelled in her chest. She arched, shaking, needing to at least tighten her thighs to relieve the pressure in her cunt, but unable to do even that much.

"All I want is the truth, Hope. Tell me what she plans." He rolled her nipple between his fingers, his grip a firm little pinch that made her desperate for more. How could she bear it? He would kill her with his touch.

"I don't know." She tossed her head in desperation.

"Tell me then what you do know," he whispered. "Tell me the names of the men who have fucked you. Tell me, Hope, so I can find some trust in you, somewhere."

She whimpered in agony.

"How can I give you what doesn't exist?" she cried out as she felt his fingers tug her hard nipple. "Wolfe, please —"

He moved closer to her then, kneeling at her breasts, moving the silk enclosed steel of his cock over her hot nipples. Hope groaned, arching into the caress. She was desperate, needing him, willing to go to any lengths to have him. She couldn't bear the arousal, so hot and deep, clenching at her cunt, making her womb spasm in need.

He moved back from her, a smile tilting his lips.

"Can you handle hours of my touch with no release, Hope?" he asked her. "I will not deny myself. I will cum, but you will not. I'll play with your pretty pussy, suck at your sweet breasts, kiss you until you are dying for the release that only I can bring you. But if you do not give me what I need, then I will be damned if I give you any measure of satisfaction."

"No," Hope wailed out, shaking her head, knowing she couldn't bear it. "I don't know, Wolfe. Don't make me lie to you, please. If you do this to me, I'll lie to you. I'll tell you anything you want to hear to make you fuck me."

"But, sweetest, I already know the truth." He bent to her, his lips outlining hers as she stared up at him in surprise.

Then her eyes closed on a ragged groan as his tongue swept into her mouth. His kiss was just as dark, just as erotic as it had been six years before. His tongue caressed hers, licking at her until she stilled it by suckling at it lightly. His moan was deep, a near growl as she drew on it. She could taste the dark spice that was uniquely his; feel her blood sing with pleasure, her heart rate increase with anticipation.

His head tilted as the kiss took on a desperate quality. He licked at her lips, nipped at them, drew her tongue into his mouth and sucked at it as he groaned torturously. Hope arched to him, her head lifting, desperate to draw him closer to her, to allow the pleasure of his kiss, his life to sink into her soul, to convince her he was here. At last she was with him. He was furious, outraged and filled with betrayed possessiveness. But he was alive, and her heart sang with the joyous knowledge.

Then he was pulling away from her, his breathing as harsh as hers, his chest rising and falling laboriously. Hope fought to understand what he was doing. Fought to make sense of why he was doing it as her body throbbed, heated and ached like a virus gone mad.

"Why are you doing this?" If he knew the answers he wanted, then why torment her in such a way?

"You betrayed me when you allowed another man entrance into what was mine," he snarled down at her. "Mine, Hope."

She licked the moisture of his kiss from her lips, nearly groaning at the erotic male essence she could literally taste.

"I didn't. But even if I had, Wolfe, you let me believe you were dead." Her breath hitched in her throat as he rose above her, his cock coming nearer to her parted lips. "You have no right to this anger, because I had no idea you were alive."

She had never tasted his erection. Had never tasted any man's. Suddenly she wanted him in her mouth, wanted to suck his cock as she had his tongue, draw on him until he couldn't help but find his release in her mouth.

He moved closer, the thick head rubbing over her lips. Hope groaned, opening her mouth for him, feeling him push into the heated depths of her mouth with a slow, measured thrust. She closed her lips on him, hearing the cry that ripped from his chest. His cock throbbed against her tongue as she laved it, her mouth suckling at it firmly.

He allowed her the freedom to suck at him, to draw the pre-cum from the small slit in his cock before he pulled back from her a second before ejaculation.

"So shy as you suck me," he whispered. "You make it hard to believe you have never had another."

"There has been no one else," she cried out. "No one, Wolfe. And you could not object if there had been. Where the hell were you?"

He shook his head, his black hair flowing over his bare shoulders.

"You knew I lived. She would have told you I lived," he replied. "You would have known I was coming for you when I could safely do so. Yet you conspired to deceive me."

He moved back and his lips went to her breast as though he could deny himself no longer, his tongue stroking over her hard nipple enticingly. He groaned roughly, his hand framing the swollen mound.

"Please," she whimpered, arching against him. She needed him to take her deep in his mouth. To suck her nipples with hard, hot draws of his lips.

He drew the small, hard tip into his mouth and began to suck it as she needed. Her groan was torn from her chest. It was so good. She could feel the pleasure traveling in a heated path to her stomach, her cunt. Both clenched in violent reaction to the hot lash of his tongue. Her vagina heated further. She could feel her juices spilling from it, coating the plump lips and soft folds that quivered for attention.

"When you are ready to tell me, Hope, then do so. Until then, I will play with your body to my heart's content. And trust me, I will find my release, without allowing you to attain your own."

Chapter Five

He moved over her body then, his lips going to her other breast, attending to it as he had the first. Hope shuddered, her body convulsing in desperate pleasure. She bucked against him; the fiery sensations assaulting her were more than she could bear. Dear God, she could never handle half an hour of this, let alone the time it would take to convince him she was telling the truth.

She whimpered as his lips traveled down her abdomen, his body settling between her spread thighs. She was open to him, her legs stretched out nearly as far as they would go, leaving her cunt vulnerable to his touch.

He licked her first. She lost her breath when his tongue swiped through the generous proof of her arousal. The syrupy juices coated her cunt, matting the tight curls and spilling down to her anus. And he was making a meal of it. He lapped at her pussy; his tongue spreading heated ecstasy as he traveled through the cream-laden slit, sucked at her swollen clit, then plunged his tongue into her vagina.

Hope screamed. Her hips came as far off the bed as the ropes would allow; desperate, shattered pleas erupted from her throat as her cunt convulsed. But he wouldn't allow the full climax. His tongue retreated as he uttered a tense chuckle, then moved to her clit. He licked it lightly, stroked it, sucked it into his mouth as she begged brokenly. Small, lightning-tinged explosions rocked her body but gave her only a small relief.

She needed to cum. She needed a mind-numbing, screaming, sanity-destroying orgasm before she disintegrated in flames. His tongue was burning her alive; the way he lapped at the juices that ran from her pussy, humming his enjoyment into her clit, stabbing his tongue deep inside her vagina.

Then his fingers were moving to her anus. Her eyes widened as one slid in slowly. She jerked against the ropes, shocked by his whisper of encouragement as he began to move the digit back and forth. Soon, another joined the first, until she felt the muscles behind stretched, fire searing her back entrance, lust rising to a crescendo that had her begging. And still he didn't stop.

He moved from her then, walking to the small bedside table as she screamed out her frustration. He lifted a tube of lubricating jelly from the drawer, his eyes heavy lidded, sensuality marking his face as he watched her. When he returned to the bottom of the bed he loosened the ropes at her feet, but the adjustment only allowed for a certain measure of movement. Then he returned to kneel between her thighs.

His fingers returned to her anus, now liberally coated with the gel. He eased her for long minutes, stretching her, preparing her, making her crazy. Then he lifted her legs until they bent over his arms as he positioned his cock.

"Did they take you here, Hope?" he whispered as the head of his cock lodged at the entrance to her ass.

He slid in before she could answer. A slow, measured thrust that had her arching to him, the bite of fire, the lance of pleasure/pain making her tighten against his erection as he slid to the hilt inside her.

She was stretched. Full. She gasped for breath, adjusting to his thick cock, fighting the licking flames of searing lust that rose to engulf her body.

"So tight," he growled, thrusting lightly. "So sweet and hot and tight, Hope."

She bucked in his arms, her head twisting against the sheets as her body tightened, pleading for more. Then his fingers were parting her cunt, sliding deep inside her, thrusting in counterpoint of his cock as he began fucking her anus.

He slid nearly free, slowly, his movements smooth and all the more arousing for it. She clenched at the retreat. The thick head nearly came free of her ass, causing her to gasp in protest. She cried and pleaded as he pushed in deep, his fingers fucking her pussy, his thumb rasping her clit.

She was close. So close. She breathed in roughly, feeling the waves building, higher, higher —

"Ah, not yet, love." His cock slid from her quickly as he moved away from the bed.

Shock held her frozen for long, agonizing minutes.

"You bastard!" she screamed out in frustration as he disappeared into the bathroom. "You perverted, rotten son of a bitch."

She would kill him, she raged. When she got free she would claw his eyes out, cut his dick off. No, on second thought she would tie him down and torture him just as he had tortured her.

"Such language," he called out as she heard water running, then shutting off. "I'll have to be certain to punish you for this as well."

He was grinning when he returned to her, his gray eyes lit with sexual mischief.

"Come, Hope, tell me what I want to know and you can climax. That's all you have to do. Just give me the answers I seek." He spread his hands mockingly before him in invitation.

"You bastard, I'll kick your ass when I get loose." She kicked at him now, but the ropes didn't allow enough room to actually touch him.

He chuckled. He lifted her legs once again, then, with his eyes locked to hers, he pushed the hot, rigid length of his cock into her weeping pussy. Hope bucked against the agonizingly slow entrance. He stretched her almost painfully, sinking his full length into her, searing her with a desire so desperate she was afraid it would destroy her.

"Please," she whimpered.

"Tell me," he demanded. "Give me what I want from you, Hope."

He pulled free of her as she screamed out a denial, then sank in with a hard, sure thrust that had her cunt gripping him hard, tightening around him, on the edge of a release so explosive she feared for her sanity. Only to pull back again, his cock slipping from her grasping, aching vagina as he lowered himself on the bed.

He stretched out between her thighs again, burying his mouth immediately in her pussy. The stunning pleasure of his tongue lapping at her, thrusting inside her, licking the sensitive walls of her cunt had her screaming out in an agony of desire. His tongue plunged inside her, licking greedily until the tremors began once again. He would move away from her then, question her again. When she had no answers he went to her breasts, sucking them, nipping at them, drawing on the sensitive nipples until she was screaming any answer she could think of. And still it wasn't what he wanted.

"Wolfe. God, I swear, Wolfe," she screamed out what seemed hours later.

Perspiration soaked her hair, trickled over her neck, between her breasts. Her throat was hoarse, tears soaked her cheeks and sobs trembled through her body. She was one huge impending orgasm. The need was desperate, her stomach cramping so badly he would have to stop, ease her through the pain, only to begin again. And again. She was mindless, unable to make sense of her surroundings, time or anything else but the desperation to climax.

"Damn you, Hope." He rose up from her body, his muscles gleaming with sweat, his expression twisted into lines of arousal. "Just tell me who fucked you. Just give me their names. That's all I ask. Just that."

She threw her head back, crying out, wailing at her inability to give him what he wanted. She had already given him names, every male name she could think of, and she still hadn't given him what he wanted.

"I swear," she screamed out desperately. "I swear, Wolfe. I swear. There was no one."

Her stomach cramped again, drawing a ragged cry of pain from her throat as he moved quickly to rub the clenched muscle with a broad hand. She breathed harshly through the charley horse-like pain. She couldn't curl her body into a better position to fight the pain, she couldn't move any more than the ropes had allowed hours before.

"Hope." He smoothed her damp hair back from her forehead, his expression indescribably gentle. "Just one name. I swear I won't hurt him. Just tell me who."

Chapter Six

Wolfe knew he couldn't hold out much longer himself. He hadn't climaxed yet, despite his earlier vow to her that he would. He suffered with her; he ached so desperately it was torture. His cock was a burning brand of need. He didn't dare push it into her mouth again, nor did he dare to fuck her tight little ass as he had earlier. He was on the edge, and he was terrified of hurting her.

He couldn't go any further. He lowered his forehead to hers, watching the tears that ran across her cheeks, wanting to cry with her. He hadn't wanted to do this to her. Not like this. But her defiance only fueled his determination to make her submit.

"Enough," he whispered, his thumb wiping away the tears, only to have more take their place.

What had happened to him? Why had he pushed her so far, tortured her in such a way with her own body? As he watched her he knew; knew to the bottom of his soul that somehow, Hope too had been betrayed. Not just by the Bitch, but now by him.

The frenzy of lust, pain and feelings of betrayal had turned him into more than an animal; he had become no better than the mother who had robbed her of her childhood, and gave her as mate to a man who was as much animal as he was human.

The "mating frenzy" was no easy thing to control, even without the intense possessiveness those pictures had inspired. It had nearly destroyed him at the labs, clawing at his gut, demanding he take her, make her his, despite her youth, her innocence. The soul-destroying evidence of those pictures showing that she had allowed another to touch her had awakened a demon inside him that he never knew existed.

"I love you," she whispered, her voice hoarse as she sobbed weakly. "I've always loved you, Wolfe. Always. I would not betray you. Please. Please fuck me."

He sighed roughly. He had the proof she would do exactly that, and yet, he could do nothing but believe her.

"If I fuck you now, Hope, I will be but an animal taking you." He couldn't do that to her. Couldn't take the chance that he would hurt her. "I don't want that. Let me leave you long enough to find my control. To be certain I will not hurt you."

Mockery twisted her exhausted expression.

"What difference does it make," she whispered, too tired to beg anymore. "Do whatever you want."

Wolfe dragged his body painfully away from her. There wasn't a chance in hell he could tolerate jeans. He jerked a pair of sweat pants from the recessed closet instead and pulled them on. His cock was a monster, straining against the material, howling for release.

Wearily, he released the ropes that bound her, then watched as she curled into a tight ball. Her back was to him then, her buttocks gleaming gently, the slick, hot entrance to her body open and clearly accessible. He clenched his teeth in agony as he jerked his shirt from the floor and tossed it to her.

"Put this on. We must talk, Hope."

"About what?" she cried out, turning to stare up at him in fury. "Let's talk about six years of hell. Of fucking grief and pain only to learn it was for nothing. Nothing, Wolfe."

He flinched at her words, but drew in a thankful breath when she rose from the bed, her body shaking from both her lust and her anger.

"Can I take a shower or do I need permission?" She ignored the shirt, standing before him, gloriously naked, furiously aroused.

"Shower," he sighed. "I will await you in the other room. We will talk then."

Or they would have. She paled dangerously, clutching her stomach and sinking back to the bed.

"Hope." He rushed to her, his hand going to her abdomen, feeling the tight bunch of muscles there that he knew would be agonizing. She panted through the pain, clutching at him, staring up at him pleadingly.

"Oh, God. Please. I'm begging you," she gasped. "It hurts, Wolfe. The arousal hurts so bad I can't bear it."

She dragged his hand to her weeping pussy, crying out, her body arching as he pushed two fingers roughly inside her. The contraction eased, her cunt tightened.

He couldn't wait a fucking hour, but more important, neither could she. He pulled away from her long enough to remove the sweat pants, then unable to control himself, he pushed her to the bed, turning her quickly to her stomach, pulling her hips up to meet his cock as he mounted her.

"No," she cried out, clawing at the sheet as he pushed her legs apart. "Please, you promised, Wolfe. You promised, no more teasing."

"No more teasing," he growled. "No more, baby. Here I am."

He plunged home with one quick, hard stroke.

Chapter Seven

Hope felt the swift invasion, the parting of flesh that had never known such a thick intrusion, the instinctive tightening of her muscles on the broad, hot cock that plunged inside her. She lost her breath; she lost any control of her body. She tilted her hips to take more, fighting for breath as he began to thrust inside her with smooth, pistoning strokes.

His erection was like a fiery brand. He fucked her with strong movements of his hips, holding hers with hard hands as he thrust inside her. The pressure, already built to unimagined heights, began to tighten further. She was so close, so close. She was terrified to attempt to give into it. If he pulled away now, she wouldn't survive.

Her cunt was one long tremor after another, the muscles convulsing, preparing for the orgasm rising to rip her apart.

"It will happen this time, baby," he swore as she tightened in preparation for him to pull back from her. "No more teasing, Hope. Cum for me baby. Let it go, because I'm going to cum for you." He thrust harder, deeper. "I'm going to fill your pussy with my seed, Hope. Cum for me, now."

She had to trust him. Her body couldn't stand it again. If he pulled away, she knew her heart would shatter. She felt her muscles begin to tighten, her pussy to throb, to convulse. Her body began to tremble in reaction as her orgasm neared. It would kill her, but she would willingly die for it.

A climax tore through her. She no longer had the energy to scream, but a low, continuing cry tore from her throat as it began. Energy hummed along her body, from her vagina, her clit, her very womb. It began to wrap around her, exploding her, destroying her. She shook from his hard thrusts, convulsing around his cock as he began to cry out with his own release.

"Fuck. No. No." She heard his bitter curse an instant before she felt the change.

Hope's eyes widened as she felt his cock harden further, and further. As though midway up that stiff stalk he was becoming even more engorged. It stretched the tight muscles of her cunt, separating them more fully. And it wasn't stopping. It kept swelling as Wolfe kept thrusting in shallow strokes, lodging it tighter and tighter inside her until he felt locked in, and the pull and tug began to trigger climax after climax as she felt his sperm begin to erupt from the tip of his cock.

Her vagina was on fire. A liquid, melting hotbed of sensations she couldn't process all at once. She was stretched further than she imagined possible; Wolfe's cock pulsing, her cunt gripping and tightening as shudder after shudder raced through her.

Wolfe was crying out behind her now. A sharp burst of heated seed would erupt, then stop. He would tug again, and another would release. Over and over, she lost count of his eruptions, and her climaxes. It continued for long, long minutes, the heat, the hard throb of blood where flesh was locked into flesh, the pump of hot semen until her body collapsed in total exhaustion, tiny orgasms still trembling through her like energized aftershocks.

Wolfe fell over her, breathing harshly, his body still jerking spasmodically as he attempted every few seconds to pull his cock from the fiery hold she had on it. Instinctively, Hope knew what was happening. It was too bizarre to be true, but she knew it could be no more than the tight swelling that accompanied canine mating. A knot formed along the cock, locking the male inside the female, ensuring that his seed was given chance to take root.

If she had the strength, she would have laughed. She should have known, as he should have known. The Feline Breeds had experienced their own animalistic qualities. The barb locked them into their female. She should have known that Wolfe, as intensely male, as dominant as he was, would bring with him his own brand of assurance.

"We're locked together, Hope." He breathed roughly, shocked, his body still shuddering in pleasure.

"Hmm, it would appear." She shivered around the hard protrusion once again.

"This has never happened before," he groaned against her shoulder, his tongue licking at the small scar that marked her as his.

She climaxed again, a soft flare of pleasure as she felt the pressure begin to recede. Then long seconds later she groaned as he pulled free, his engorged dick stimulating her sensitive vagina.

He fell onto the bed beside her, breathing roughly. His arms dragged her against him, holding her tight to his chest as his lips pressed against her forehead, caressed her cheek, then settled roughly on hers. He kissed her, not as a man starved to possess, but as one desperate for atonement.

Her lips opened to his, gentling him. Their tongues twined together, then slid apart as he raised his head to stare down at her.

"I nearly went mad without you," he whispered, breaking her heart with the pain in his voice and in his eyes. "I knew you were safe the day the labs were overrun. I set the explosions in the cells and ran with the others. I had to get them to safety, ensure their lives before I could come for you."

She pressed her lips together as she fought her pain and her tears.

"I thought I had lost you forever." She touched his lips with trembling fingers. "I merely existed, Wolfe. I would have preferred to fight the fight with you. To have been a part of your freedom. All of it."

He shook his head. "I could risk our lives because I had to. Not yours. You were too important to me, Hope. Without you, I had nothing. No prayer, no hope of ever attaining happiness. You are my hope. All of it."

A tear slid from her eye, only to be caught by his calloused thumb.

"You are free now." He grinned. "Are you still going to kick my ass?"

Hope breathed out in a weak attempt at laughter.

"I'm going to kick it really hard as soon as I get my breath," she assured him. "Next time, I get to tie you up, and let you see how it feels."

His eyes flared with a measure of worry. She considered it for long moments, knowing he would do it, for her. She finally shrugged. "Hell, I guess you need your hands free, huh?"

"It would make it much easier to love you," he assured her with dark promise as his hands caressed her back, twined in her long black hair. "And I can love you well, my Hope."

"Tell me what happened." She needed to know why it had taken him so long to come for her.

Wolfe sighed deeply.

"When we escaped, it was with no money, no supplies, nothing but our instincts." He shrugged heavily, grimacing at the thought of those early days. "We barely survived before I was able to arm us and train the males sufficiently to fight. Then we began hiring ourselves out. Kidnappings, search and rescue. A few stints as hired guns in petty wars. Our reputation didn't take long to grow. We computerized, took only the assignments we were assured were not tricks of your mother's, and grew more secure."

"When did she find you?" She needed to know how long her mother had allowed her to live, grief-stricken, in pain without him.

"Within two years. She made her first attempt to recapture us through a kidnapping she arranged. When that didn't work, she began sending me pictures of you. Last year I received several, via my Internet connection, of you with several other men. I went insane, Hope."

His simple words vibrated with agony and loss.

"I visit the gynecologist monthly, because of the effects of the 'mating'," she told him hesitantly. "Last month, I was sore, hurting afterwards. She must have had him rupture the hymen to ensure your belief in it."

Would he believe her? She stared up at his quiet face, seeing none of the disgust, the fury that had been there earlier.

He shook his head. "I should have known. I should have thought. But all I could think about was another touching you. I have not been stable these last months, beloved." He kissed her lips gently, an apology, an unspoken plea in his eyes that she forgive him. And she could do no less.

"Well, after such incredible orgasms, I guess I can forgive you," she whispered with a sensual smile. She was more than ready for another.

Hope frowned then as his eyes closed with weary resignation, and though he appeared relaxed, she could see his muscles slowly tightening as though his body was preparing for a blow. His arms tightened around her as he took a harsh breath a second before she heard her mother's sneering voice.

"So it would appear the animal has made an appearance. You knotted her good, Wolfe. You should be proud. I'll enjoy training your brats to obey me a bit better than you did though."

Terror shot through Hope. She turned to roll from beneath him, to keep him from sheltering her body with his own, but he controlled the movement with a tightening of his arms around her.

"I love you, Hope," he whispered a second before he raised his head, staring in cold fury at the woman who had invaded his life once again as she leaned casually against the framed doorway.

Chapter Eight

"Hello, Bitch. Why am I not surprised to see you here?" His voice was filled with disgust at the vision he saw before him.

Wolfe looked over at the small, diminutive woman who stepped into the room. She was dressed casually in a pullover sweater, twill pants and loafers. The very picture of a successful doctor, if you discounted the lethal pistol in her hand, and the gleam of vicious triumph in her black eyes.

"I knew the altered pictures of those men fucking her would bring you out," she chortled gleefully. "Did you really think my frigid daughter would allow one man to touch her, let alone two at a time? Her doctor had to rupture her hymen, she was so damned cold. Really, Wolfe, you two made it frighteningly easy to capture you."

He smiled. The trap was sprung, just as he had anticipated. But he was more than thankful to the monster for clearing up the matter of his sole possession of Hope.

"Yeah, I did, didn't I? Perhaps you were the easy one though," he suggested with a smile.

Delia Bainesmith's eyes narrowed.

"You always were a rogue," she sneered. "Never obeying orders, always attempting to escape. You were mine. My animal, my possession. I created you."

Her voice echoed with her fury, her insane belief that he should always be in her control.

"You created me, but you will never own me," he promised her lethally. "You forget, Bitch. You used the DNA of a wolf, not the lap puppies you should have. No man or woman controls the wolf."

"Then I will control the whelps you've bred on my traitorous daughter," she sneered, raising the gun, her finger tightening on the trigger. "And I'll kill you."

He flipped the switch on the wall behind him before she could react. The gun flew from her hand, clattering over the floor as she was knocked off balance by the falling sandbag and imploding plaster from the ceiling.

It was the opening he needed. Wolfe jumped from the bed, reaching down for the gun as she flew at him, a dagger in her hand, maniacal hatred contorting her expression. He heard Hope cry his name out in fear, her voice filled with tears, with terror. He flung himself away from the monster, angling one leg out in a quick, arching motion, taking a swipe at her feet as she passed by. A startled cry erupted from her throat as she fell.

Wolfe jumped to his feet, gripping the gun as he pointed it at her, watching her carefully. It was then he saw the blood oozing slowly from beneath her body. Hope must have seen it as well. He heard her breath catch, glimpsed her pale, horrified face.

He went to the scientist, once the terror of the labs he had been confined to. He turned her over carefully, grimacing at the sight of the dagger lodged between her breasts.

"Bastard." Blood bubbled from her mouth as she stared at him in hatred. "Ruined it. You ruined it all."

Wolfe glanced up at Hope. Shock lined her expression, wiping all color from her face. The woman's gaze followed his. She sneered at the child she had borne.

"Animal. No better than a dog—" she gasped. Her eyes widened, then dimmed.

"Wolfe." The others were rushing through the cabin now, voices raised in fear. "Wolfe, dammit, she got by us—"

They came to a sudden halt inside the bedroom. The three women and three men, all out of breath, were smeared with blood, but triumphant.

"Did you get the soldiers?" Wolfe asked them quietly as he moved to Hope, drawing the blanket around her silent body as he picked her up from the bed.

"All of them," Jacob reported. "We didn't kill them though." He nodded to the still form of the scientist.

"Get her out of here," he ordered them. "Find a deep, dark hole and bury the bitch in it. She won't get a chance to hurt anyone else."

He carried Hope into the living room, sheltering her body with his as he felt her low sobs against his chest.

"I won't grieve for her," she whispered tearfully. "I did that when I was a child."

"It's okay to grieve, Hope," he assured her sadly. "Grieve for what never was if you need to. But let it go."

He sat down on the couch, cradling her to him.

"She would have killed you," she whispered. "She would have killed me as well, eventually."

He smoothed her hair back from her face, grieving for her.

"Can you forgive me for her death? Forgive me for what I put you through? For not trusting you?" He touched her with adoration, with pain, with thanksgiving.

For a moment her expression went blank, then a most curious light of female knowledge lit her eyes.

Wolfe narrowed his eyes on her.

"What?" he asked her.

"I climaxed," she whispered.

He grinned. "Yes, you did. Quite well, too."

"No." She shook her head. "While you thought you were torturing me, those screams of agony were actually orgasms. Not big ones, but enough."

He frowned. "That's not possible. Do not try to salve my conscience, Hope."

She laughed. She dared to laugh in his face.

"Want to try it again in a few days, so I can prove it?" she offered.

Heat flared in his body. His cock hardened.

"Do I get to tie you up again?" he asked her, definitely interested.

She shrugged. "If you want to." But he could see the excitement in her eyes.

Wolfe sighed deeply. "Why do I get the feeling, Hope, that you have effectively turned the tables on me without my knowledge?"

Her sapphire eyes gleamed up at him.

"Maybe because I did. And I won't grieve over her, Wolfe. I was more terrified for you. I thought for certain she would hurt you. Maybe kill you. I couldn't live with it, if she had. I would have died with you."

He touched his lips to hers as he stared into her eyes.

"I love you," he whispered against the tender curves. "Always, Hope. I will always love you."

Her eyes drifted closed on a drowsy sigh of contentment. He held her tightly to his chest, thanking God every second that she was safe, that the Bitch was dead. Their lives would be safe now, and he needed that for her.

"Wolfe." Jacob stood beside him, watching him quietly. "We're going to take her body back to her soldiers. When they awaken, they can do whatever the hell they want to with her."

"Did they find the cabin as well?" He couldn't risk that knowledge.

"Hell, they didn't make it ten feet from the truck. The Bitch wouldn't have found it if you hadn't left orders to let her through."

Wolfe nodded. He hadn't meant to kill her, but he knew they were all better off with her death.

"We will leave you with your woman then. When should we return?" Amusement lit Jacob's light blue eyes.

Wolfe grinned. "Weeks perhaps," he answered him tiredly. "I have time to make up for, my friend. Several years at least."

Hope slept in his arms, unaware of her mother's body being carted out of the cabin. As the door closed behind Jacob and the others, he sighed deeply. He had his Hope, just as he had always dreamed of, prayed for. His life would now be complete.

* * * * *

Jacob refused to look back at the couple as he left the cabin. Anger and need rode him hard, arousal was a steady beat of blood in his cock to torment and torture him. But it wasn't the woman Wolfe held that kept Jacob's dick in a constant state of readiness. It was the one who awaited him outside.

As he closed the door behind him, Faith moved from her position at the end of the house, her black eyes watching him warily as he stalked toward her. She was a wolf breed, the slender, compact lines of her body were lightly muscular, her breasts high and firm beneath the black t-shirt she wore with black jeans. Her reddish brown hair was a raggedly cut cap of silk and framed her slender face in a way that gave her a vulnerable, untouchable look.

"They're all right?" she asked as he neared her.

Jacob growled, baring his teeth in warning as she stepped back from him. She was always stepping back, never forward.

"Were they not, you would have known," he said, furious with her once again.

"Well, bite me, why don't you," she snapped, her brows lowering in a frown. "It was a reasonable question."

"From a most unreasonable female," he accused her harshly. "Return to the cabin and rest. You have not slept in days and I'm tired of the shadows under your eyes."

"You rest." Her body came to attention immediately, anger pulsing through her, scenting the air. "Do I tell you how often to sleep?"

He turned to her, fighting the need to reach out to her, to drag her to him.

"Do as I said," he snapped.

"Fuck you, Jake, you go to sleep…"

"Do not worry, the day will come when you will do just that, Faith. Until you can handle it, I suggest you run now, and run fast, or you may learn what it feels like to have your mate mount you without your permission." Fury snapped in his body. Her continued defiance roused the beast and made it howl.

He watched her pale. Terror flashed in her eyes a second before she ran. He cursed violently, dragging his hands through his hair as he tamped down the beast that demanded he run her down. He couldn't. He never could. She was his mate, and yet he would be forever denied her touch. His ravenous, grieving howl echoed through the mountains now, as it echoed through his soul.

The End

About the author:

Lora Leigh is a 36-year-old wife and mother living in Kentucky. She dreams in bright, vivid images of the characters intent on taking over her writing life, and fights a constant battle to put them on the hard drive of her computer before they can disappear as fast as they appeared. Lora's family, and her writing life co-exist, if not in harmony, in relative peace with each other. An understanding husband is the key to late nights with difficult scenes, and stubborn characters. His insights into human nature, and the workings of the male psyche provide her hours of laughter, and innumerable romantic ideas that she works tirelessly to put into effect.

Lora welcomes mail from readers. You can write to her c/o Ellora's Cave Publishing at 1337 Commerce Drive, Suite 13, Stow OH 44224.

Also by Lora Leigh:

Why an electronic book?

We live in the Information Age — an exciting time in the history of human civilization in which technology rules supreme and continues to progress in leaps and bounds every minute of every hour of every day. For a multitude of reasons, more and more avid literary fans are opting to purchase e-books instead of paperbacks. The question to those not yet initiated to the world of electronic reading is simply: *why?*

1. *Price.* An electronic title at Ellora's Cave Publishing runs anywhere from 40-75% less than the cover price of the <u>exact same title</u> in paperback format. Why? Cold mathematics. It is less expensive to publish an e-book than it is to publish a paperback, so the savings are passed along to the consumer.

2. *Space.* Running out of room to house your paperback books? That is one worry you will never have with electronic novels. For a low one-time cost, you can purchase a handheld computer designed specifically for e-reading purposes. Many e-readers are larger than the average handheld, giving you plenty of screen room. Better yet, hundreds of titles can be stored within your new library — a single microchip. (Please note that Ellora's Cave does not endorse any specific brands. You can check

our website at www.ellorascave.com for customer recommendations we make available to new consumers.)

3. *Mobility.* Because your new library now consists of only a microchip, your entire cache of books can be taken with you wherever you go.

4. *Personal preferences are accounted for.* Are the words you are currently reading too small? Too large? Too...**ANNOYING**? Paperback books cannot be modified according to personal preferences, but e-books can.

5. *Innovation.* The way you read a book is not the only advancement the Information Age has gifted the literary community with. There is also the factor of what you can read. Ellora's Cave Publishing will be introducing a new line of interactive titles that are available in e-book format only.

6. *Instant gratification.* Is it the middle of the night and all the bookstores are closed? Are you tired of waiting days—sometimes weeks—for online and offline bookstores to ship the novels you bought? Ellora's Cave Publishing sells instantaneous downloads 24 hours a day, 7 days a week, 365 days a year. Our e-book delivery system is 100% automated, meaning your order is filled as soon as you pay for it.

Those are a few of the top reasons why electronic novels are displacing paperbacks for many an avid reader. As always, Ellora's Cave Publishing welcomes your questions and comments. We invite you to email us at service@ellorascave.com or write to us directly at: P.O. Box 787, Hudson, Ohio 44236-0787.

LaVergne, TN USA
01 October 2009
159630LV00001B/9/A